Smiling broadly, he gently patted her cheek. "This is great, Sophia. I knew you'd be perfect at this gift-finding thing."

His praise sent a shot of joy through her and she laughed softly. "I got lucky, that's all."

He wrapped his hand around her upper arm and Sophia couldn't ignore the warmth that radiated from his fingers, down through the fabric of her blouse, all the way to her flesh.

"So did I," he said.

Confused by his remark, she looked up at him. "What do you mean? Lucky that you managed to find three gifts in one store?"

He gave a low chuckle. "No. I'm lucky to have you with me tonight."

Of course he was teasing, she told herself. Yet even knowing that, the twinkle in his dark eyes was enough to make her heart beat faster.

Purposely making her voice light and playful, she said, "Before the night is over you might start regretting my company."

He urged her in the direction of the checkout counter. "Don't worry. I'll tell you if you're giving me a headache."

Headache? Heartache? There was little doubt in Sophia's mind that Colt could give her both of those woes. If she let him.

Dear Reader,

When the Christmas season rolls around on Three Rivers Ranch nothing is held back. Not with the merrymaking, or the cost of transforming the ranch into a magical wonderland. Decorated spruce trees are erected throughout the house, while loads of rich food and desserts flow from the kitchen. Even the cattle and horse barns are decorated with evergreens and huge red ribbons.

For horse trainer Colt Crawford, this will be his first Christmas on the ranch; however, he's not planning to join in on all the partying. After becoming disillusioned with dating, he's decided to take a break from women. Spending a quiet holiday with his brother, sister-in-law and baby nephew will be more than enough excitement for him.

But Colt's way of thinking is suddenly changed when a pretty Christmas elf with dark brown hair and brown eyes shows up at the horse barn with a box of holiday treats. One look at her and Colt is convinced she'd make his Christmas a whole lot sweeter!

Less than a month has passed since Sophia Vandale took the job as cook for the Hollisters. Leaving California behind, she's come to the ranch to forget her broken engagement and the chance she lost to have a family of her own. The last thing she needs in her life is a handsome cowboy with a smile hot enough to warm the coldest winter night...

I hope you'll join me and the Hollisters as we celebrate the holidays. And may your Christmas be filled with cheer and much love!

Merry Christmas!

Stella Bagwell

Sleigh Ride
with the Rancher

STELLA BAGWELL

HARLEQUIN®
SPECIAL EDITION™

Recycling programs
for this product may
not exist in your area.

ISBN-13: 978-1-335-40822-8

Sleigh Ride with the Rancher

Copyright © 2021 by Stella Bagwell

For questions and comments about the quality of this book, please contact us at CustomerService@Harlequin.com.

Harlequin Enterprises ULC
22 Adelaide St. West, 40th Floor
Toronto, Ontario M5H 4E3, Canada
www.Harlequin.com

Printed in U.S.A.

After writing more than one hundred books for Harlequin, **Stella Bagwell** still finds it exciting to create new stories and bring her characters to life. She loves all things Western and has been married to her own real cowboy for forty-four years. Living on the south Texas coast, she also enjoys being outdoors and helping her husband care for the horses, cats and dog that call their small ranch home. The couple has one son, who teaches high school mathematics and is also an athletic director. Stella loves hearing from readers. They can contact her at stellabagwell@gmail.com.

Books by Stella Bagwell

Harlequin Special Edition

Men of the West

His Texas Runaway
Home to Blue Stallion Ranch
The Rancher's Best Gift
Her Man Behind the Badge
His Forever Texas Rose
The Baby That Binds Them

Montana Mavericks: The Real Cowboys of Bronco Heights

For His Daughter's Sake

The Fortunes of Texas: The Lost Fortunes

Guarding His Fortune

Montana Mavericks: The Lonelyhearts Ranch

The Little Maverick Matchmaker

Visit the Author Profile page
at Harlequin.com for more titles.

To my husband, Harrell.
Thank you, darling, for making every day of the year
feel like Christmas to me!

Chapter One

"Whoa! Look at this! One of Santa's helpers is making an early visit to the barn this morning!"

Halting in his tracks, Colt Crawford peered toward the opposite end of the horse barn, where a young woman with dark hair and fuzzy red earmuffs was handing out food from a cardboard box.

From a few feet behind him, Colt's older brother, Luke, commented, "Last time I looked Sophia Vandale worked in the ranch house kitchen. Not for Santa at the North Pole."

Since Colt had taken over the job of barn manager for the Hollister family on Three Rivers Ranch, he'd visited the big ranch house a few times. But he didn't remember seeing this woman during any of those visits, or recall hearing the name Sophia. But the ranch was massive, and even after three months of working here, Colt was still trying to remember the names of all the hands.

"Jazelle is the only woman I've seen bring food to the barn," Colt commented as he continued to gaze at the female visitor. "Is this someone new?"

Luke faked a cough. "I thought you'd gone on a fasting diet. No women. No dates. Remember?"

Glancing over his shoulder, Colt frowned at his brother. "It doesn't hurt for a man to look, does it?"

"Sophia is Reeva's granddaughter," Luke said as he proceeded to unsaddle the horse he'd been exercising. "She's working in the kitchen with her."

"You mean the house cook? This is her granddaughter?"

"Yep."

Colt glanced back to where the woman was still surrounded by barn workers. Even though he could only glimpse parts of her, he could see enough to spark his interest. "Come on," he told Luke. "Let's go get some of what she's passing out."

"You go on," Luke told him. "Pru fixed breakfast tacos before she left for school. I'm still full."

At times it was still hard for Colt to remember his brother was now a happily married man with a baby son. The two men had been bachelors together until Luke had moved here to Three Rivers and found his soul mate. Colt was happy for his brother, but he had no desire to follow in his footsteps. No, Colt was content to be footloose, and he had every intention of remaining that way.

Colt led the horse he'd been riding up to a wooden hitching rail and tied off the lead rope. "Well, my breakfast was a piece of toast washed down with a cup of coffee," he told Luke. "I'm hungry."

The December morning was cold, especially for this part of Arizona. In spite of the infrared heaters hanging over certain areas of the massive barn, the air was still chilly enough to turn his breath into a vapor cloud as he strode down the wide alleyway. Obviously, the woman called Sophia had anticipated the barn being cold. Now that Colt was almost upon the group, he could see she was wearing a puffy red nylon jacket that matched the earmuffs.

As Colt worked his way through the circle of men, an older groom by the name of Riggs spotted him and waved. "Hey, Colt, try the cookies. They're great. And the fudge, too."

Colt gave the older man a thumbs-up for the advice, then inched his way forward to where the woman had balanced the weight of the loaded box on top of a hitching rail.

She looked around just as he came to a halt near her left side, and as their gazes met, Colt felt a wave of heat wash over him. The sensation almost had him glancing up to the rafters to see if a new heater had been installed on this end of the building. But since he was the barn manager, he knew everything that came and went through the doors. Besides, it was much easier to keep his attention on her, he thought, while the warmth that had generated somewhere inside him made a mad dash to his face.

"I hope the men left something for me," he said to her.

She smiled, and Colt instantly decided she had to be a Christmas fairy. Why else would her brown eyes be twinkling and her whole face radiating a special glow?

"You've missed the doughnuts," she told him. "But there are plenty of cookies, fudge and toffee left."

Gauging her age to be a few years younger than Colt's thirty, he noted she had coal-black hair that waved gently against an oval-shaped face. Her olive complexion was as smooth as the petal of a rose, while the warm brown eyes gazing back at him were set beneath a pair of delicate black brows and fringed with long black lashes. Her plush lips were the color of pink that lit the sky right before sundown, and to his delight, they were curved into a charming smile directed straight at him.

Colt wanted to tell her she looked as scrumptious as a Christmas cookie, but he clamped down on the flirtatious thought. Since they'd never met before, he hardly wanted to give her the idea that he was a sleazy creep.

"Get one of everything," Jim, the head wrangler who worked closely with Luke, told him. "It's the holiday season. We're supposed to eat too much of all the good things."

Colt chuckled at the man's suggestion. "I'll go along with that."

Sophia handed him a napkin and a paper plate. "Go ahead," she urged Colt. "Pick out whatever you'd like."

"Thanks." Colt promptly began to pile cookies and candy on the plate, while trying to keep his eyes on the sweet treats rather than her. "Did you make these things?"

"I baked the cookies. My grandmother made the candy. It takes a little more finesse than I've acquired—so far."

She had a rich voice that matched the vivid colors of her hair and face. Colt found he was drawn to the sound as much as he was to her smile.

Finished with filling his plate, he covered the goodies with the napkin she'd given him and eased back from the rail.

"This all looks delicious," he told her. "I know the guys appreciate your thoughtfulness of treating us with this home cooking. So do I."

He didn't know when or how it had happened, but in the last minute or two, the cowboys who'd been standing around munching cookies and candy had seemed to vanish to other areas of the barn.

As he glanced around in surprise, she said, "They must've all decided it was time to go back to work. I guess I should apologize for interrupting your day. But Maureen sent me down here. I think she likes spoiling you guys," she added with another smile. "Uh, by the way, my name is Sophia Vandale. Reeva is my grandmother."

He extended his hand to her. "I'm Colt Crawford. Nice to meet you, Sophia."

She pulled her hand from her coat pocket and placed it in his. Luke was surprised by the warmth of her skin and the firmness of her grip.

"Are you related to Luke?" she asked.

"I'm his younger brother. Do you know him?"

"I only met him a few days ago," she said. "He and his wife and baby came by the ranch house the other evening to chat with Blake and Kat."

He grinned at her. "I see. Well, Luke is just as nice as me."

She grinned back at him, and Colt felt the ridiculous urge to do a happy jig.

"Or vice versa?"

"Right." He darted a swift glance over his shoulder to see Luke and the horse he'd been unsaddling had disappeared. However, several hands were already back to mucking stalls and filling hay mangers. On sudden impulse he said, "Uh, before you leave, why don't we walk down to Holt's office and enjoy these cookies together?"

Surprise and doubt swirled together and swept across her face. "Oh, I probably shouldn't. Gran will be needing me."

He didn't know why he'd suddenly been struck with the urge to talk to this woman. Sure, she was pretty, and she wasn't wearing any type of ring, but he'd been steering clear of women for a good reason. His life was stress-free without them. But what the heck? A few minutes with Sophia was hardly going to cause the roof to crash in on him.

He said, "Surely, Reeva can manage on her own long enough for you to eat a cookie, and Jazelle brought a thermos of coffee to the office earlier. It should still be hot."

She hesitated for a moment longer before she nodded in concession. "Okay. But I can't dally long."

"Now you're talking. Just follow me. But watch your step. The men try to keep most of the manure out of the alleyway, but there's always a few piles around."

She lifted the box of sweets and stepped to his side. Colt had already noticed that beneath the puffy jacket and black skinny jeans she had a slender build. But now that she was standing next to him, he realized she'd probably have to stand on her tiptoes for the top of her head to even reach the middle of his chest. Not that she'd ever be *that* close to him, he thought.

"No worries," she told him. "I'm wearing boots, and they can be cleaned easily enough."

Suddenly remembering his manners, he said, "Here, I'll trade you. You carry my plate, and I'll carry your box."

"It's not very heavy. I can manage. Unless you just insist."

"I do."

They made the switch, then started walking in the direction of Holt's office. Along the way, stalled horses whinnied and stomped, while the pungent smell of alfalfa hay mixed with the scents of manure and pine shavings. Blocks of sunshine streaming through the skylights in the roof illuminated particles of dust and bits of hay flying through the air. Somewhere in the distance, the sound of a radio competed with a pair of dogs barking just outside the barn door.

The sights and sounds were as familiar to Colt as the back of his hand. His first memories were those of horses and barns and tagging behind his father and brother. This was his world, and though he sometimes visited other places, he never ventured far from his domain.

"Won't we be interrupting Holt?" Sophia asked as they neared the door to the office. "I understand he manages the horse division and is a very busy man."

"You're right. He's extremely busy. But he won't be here until later today. This morning he's helping his wife, Isabelle, with some of the mares on Blue

Stallion Ranch. That's her horse ranch—well, it's the ranch she bought and built on her own," he felt compelled to explain. "Now she and Holt run the ranch together. But you've probably already learned about the Hollisters."

"My grandmother might've explained to me about Blue Stallion. I can't remember. Since I moved here, I've had so much information thrown at me about the Hollister family. Sometimes I struggle to keep it all straight."

"You're not alone," he told her. "I'm still learning who's who around here and the names of their wives and kids."

He opened a door made of heavy boards and motioned for Sophia to precede him into a large space with the same open ceiling as the working area of the barn. Both the walls and the floor were made of rough two-by-eight boards that had turned to a muted gray color over the years. On one side, the room was furnished with a wooden desk, a leather executive chair and a row of metal filing cabinets. Three straight-backed wooden chairs were situated in front of the desk, while a green leather couch and a small table with a coffee brewer lined the opposite wall. A strip of fluorescent lighting hung from the rafters and illuminated the desk area.

"Sit wherever you'd like," Colt told her as he carried the box of sweets over to the refreshment table.

"I'll get us a cup of coffee. Do you take cream or sugar?"

"Both, thanks."

She sat down in one of the chairs and positioned her feet toward the electric space heater blowing in the direction of the desk area. Colt poured the coffee and after adding the cream and sugar to hers, carried them over to where she was sitting.

"I put your plate on the desk," she said, as she accepted the coffee from him.

He took the chair closest to hers and reached for the plate of cookies. "You came at just the right time," he said. "I was needing a break. I've been here at the barn since five this morning and hadn't stopped for coffee until now."

He extended the plate toward her, but she shook her head. "Thanks, but I've already had a cookie when I took them out of the oven."

"Then take a piece of candy," he urged. "You need something to go with your coffee."

She shot him an amused look. "What are you around here, anyway? A salesman?"

He chuckled. "Heck no. Why would you ask such a question?"

"Because you're doing your best to convince me that I need to eat something. And doing a fairly good job of it," she added, as she lifted a piece of divinity candy from the plate.

"Well, I believe everything tastes better when

you have someone eating with you," he reasoned. "As for a salesman, Holt is the man who does all the buying and selling around here. And he's an expert at it."

She bit into the divinity and followed it with a sip of coffee. Colt was so busy watching her, he almost forgot he was supposed to be eating, too.

"So what do you do around here?" she asked. "You help take care of the horses?"

"In a way. I'm the barn manager—for the horse barn, that is. I make sure everything is running smoothly and that the horses are well and have all their needs met."

"I have a feeling you do more than that," she said.

Her remark surprised him. "Actually, on most days I do a multitude of things. I even help Holt and Luke with the training. That's what I mainly did before I moved here to Three Rivers—I trained horses for riding, roping, ranch work—that sort of thing."

"Oh. So when did you come here to Three Rivers?"

He bit into one of the cookies and discovered it was delicious. "The first week of September. I worked on a ranch near Clovis, New Mexico, before."

"I'm from California. I've only been here a couple of weeks, so you've been here nearly three months longer than I have."

"Hmm. That means we have something in common. We're both new to Three Rivers Ranch."

She nodded. "How do you like it here?"

"Couldn't be better. The Hollisters are great folks. The ranch is unbelievably beautiful, and my job is everything I love. What about you?"

Colt found himself staring at the curved corners of her lips and wondering if they might taste sweeter than the cookie he was eating.

What's the matter with you, Colt? You met this woman not more than ten minutes ago, and already you're daydreaming about kissing her? Better slap yourself awake, cowboy. That kind of thinking will lead you straight to trouble.

"I was expecting it to be great. But it's even better than I anticipated. Working with my grandmother is the best," she said, then followed her words with a light laugh. "People who know Reeva would probably roll their eyes at the idea she'd be easy to work with. She can be cranky and stern, but on the inside she's a real cream puff. And she'd never ask me to do more than what she can do."

"So I'm going to assume you like to cook. Is that what you did back in California?"

His question caused her to laugh outright and he looked at her with puzzled amusement.

"Was my question that funny?" he asked.

"It was hilarious. But you'd have to be me to understand. I used to be an interior designer for a contractor in the Los Angeles area. And I was drowning in work, I might add."

He shook his head in disbelief. Now here she sat in a room that used to store riding tack. The floor rarely saw a broom, and dusty cobwebs hung from the rafters. At one time there used to be a window to one side of the door, but after a horse kicked off a shoe and the piece of iron flew through the glass, Holt had it covered with a piece of plywood. Colt could only wonder what she thought about her surroundings.

"An interior designer, huh? You mean you pointed out where a painting should be hung on the wall or a table should be placed in a room?"

She laughed again, and Colt was glad that, at least, he wasn't offending her.

"Not exactly," she said with a smile.

"To be honest, the only thing I know about an interior designer is what I've seen in the movies. I guess you're probably thinking Holt's office could use quite a bit of help."

Smiling, she looked curiously around her. "Not really. Obviously the Hollisters are wealthy enough to have all kinds of lavish offices, but it's clear that Holt feels comfortable here in the barn and close to his horses. And over the years I've learned that the most important thing is for a person to feel comfortable and at home in their surroundings."

"Shows you how much I know about interior design. I thought it was all about making things look good."

"Well, looking good can go along with being comfortable." She leveled her gaze on his face. "So have you always been a horseman?"

He nodded as he swallowed a piece of the rich fudge. "My father carried us two boys around on a horse before we could walk. And both of us grew up loving the animals. In the beginning none of us made much money at training. It's a trade you have to build. But I've always been a believer of working at something you love and it won't ever feel like work." He shrugged and chuckled. "Whether you ever make a good living at it is another matter."

She continued to study him thoughtfully, and Colt wondered if she was as curious about him as he was about her. No. He couldn't imagine that. Because right at this moment, he could ask her dozens of questions. He could sit here for hours just listening to her voice and watching the subtle changes in her expressions as she spoke. Her eyes said as much as her words, and he found himself watching the brown orbs even more than the movement of her lips.

"So does your father work here on the ranch, too?" she asked.

"No. He's back in Texas and trains for a big ranch in Deaf Smith County. It'd be nice if he was here. But he'd never leave Texas. That's where his roots are, and you know how older people are. They get set in their ways."

Her brows arched slightly. "Your father is an older gentleman?"

He laughed at her description. "He'd kick my rear if he heard me call him *old*. Let's see, I think he turned fifty-seven about a month ago."

"My grandmother, Reeva, would call him a young rooster. She's in her early seventies and considers herself still young." She gave him an impish smile, then asked, "What about your mom? Is she into horses, too?"

Colt took a long sip of coffee before he answered. "No. She never was much of an outdoor person."

"Was?"

He did his best not to grimace. "She was killed in a highway accident when Luke and I were teenagers. Dad never remarried. What about your parents? Do they live around here?"

With a slight shake of her head, she looked away from him. "My parents split when I was only two. Dad lives close to Sacramento. And Mom lives in LA. She and my grandmother are…estranged. But that's a whole other matter. If you ever have a few spare hours," she joked, "I'll tell you about it. But it's December, Christmas is coming. This is a time to be cheerful."

"Maureen has sent word to us that she's getting all the decorations ready to be sent down to the barns," Colt said. "From what I understand, even the cattle barns get decked out in evergreen and red bows."

She laughed softly. "I wonder if the livestock appreciate the decorations?"

He chuckled. "Since this is my first Christmas on Three Rivers I couldn't say. Luke tells me everything is draped and hung so that the horses or the cattle can't get their mouths on anything. And no mistletoe is allowed in the barns. It's poisonous to animals."

"It's kind of dangerous to humans, too," she suggested. "In more ways than one."

The sudden need to clear his throat had him swigging down a gulp of coffee. "Uh...yeah. A person needs to be careful around a sprig of mistletoe."

Was that faint curve to her lips a suggestive smile, or was she simply amused? With a line puckering the skin between her brows, it was impossible to tell. How could a woman smile and frown at the same time? And why did he find everything about her so enchanting?

The questions were rolling through his thoughts when she suddenly rose to her feet and dropped the foam cup into a trash can at the side of the desk.

"It's been nice chatting with you, Colt. But it's time for me to get back to the house."

The disappointment that coursed through him made him feel like an idiot. He didn't have time to sit around flirting—or he should probably think of it as *attempting* to flirt—with a pretty woman. He had work to do.

Leaving the chair, he walked over and retrieved the box of candy and cookies. "Let me carry this out of the barn for you," he offered. "Or better yet, I can drive you back to the ranch house."

"Thanks, but I drove one of the ranch trucks down here to the barn. I'll drive it back to the house. And the box of goodies stays here," she told him. "Once Holt takes what he wants, you might pass the leftovers to the rest of the guys. The food is a Christmas gift, and after you give a gift you shouldn't take part of it back."

He returned the box to the table and turned a smile on her. "I'll try to remember that little lesson. And I'll say thanks for all the men."

"I'll be sure and give Maureen and Gran your appreciation."

She walked over to the door, and Colt quickly joined her.

"I'll walk you out," he told her. "And you can look at the horses along the way. Do you like horses?"

"Love them. But the only time I've ever been around them is when I've visited the ranch," she confessed. "So my knowledge about them is very limited."

They stepped out of the office, and after he fastened the door, the two of them began to walk side by side toward the west end of the building.

"Have you ever ridden a horse?" Colt asked.

She chuckled. "My last visit here I let Hannah—

that's Vivian's teenage daughter in case you don't know—talk me into climbing on a horse."

"Yes, I've met Hannah. She's quite a little horse-woman. I'm sure she gave you plenty of good instructions."

"Instructions? Are you kidding? I was so terrified I could hardly focus on what she was telling me. Anyway, she led the animal around, and all I had to do was hang on. Fortunately I didn't fall off. Because, let me tell you, from where I was sitting, the ground looked like it was a mile away."

"You overestimated," he teased. "Depending on the size of the horse, the ground probably wasn't more than three-quarters of a mile away."

Another laugh passed her lips, and Colt decided he could get used to the sound. It wasn't an annoying giggle like the girls he'd dated back in New Mexico. It was a natural, throaty expression that he found totally sexy.

"A mile or three-quarters. Either one would break a bone. With my luck it would probably be my neck," she joked, then halted her steps as she pointed to a palomino stallion hanging his head over the stall gate. "That's a gorgeous horse. Do you ride him?"

Colt paused at her side. "He's ridden only occasionally for exercise. His job is to, uh, produce yellow foals."

She glanced curiously up at him. "Forgive my

ignorance, but is there a reason you want that certain color?"

"Sure. People like them."

She made a face at his simple answer. "Okay. Do his babies turn out to be palominos?"

"It's still too early to predict the percentage of yellow babies he'll have. Holt only purchased the stallion last fall, and at that time Luke hauled him all the way home from Reno, Nevada. His first crop of foals is just now beginning to drop, and so far two out of three have been yellow. That's a good sign."

She gazed thoughtfully at the stallion who was bobbing his head at the two of them. "Oh my, how long do mares gestate? Must be a long time."

"Somewhere around eleven months and twenty days," Colt answered. "Sometimes less. Sometimes more. There are a few mares who go past a year."

"Hmm. A long time to wait and watch—and hope."

The wistful note in her voice brought Colt's gaze to her face, and he got the impression that she was thinking about something far different than mares and foals. But that was her business, he told himself. Not his.

"Well, you know the old saying about good things coming to those who wait," he said.

She looked up at him and smiled. "And right now Gran is probably waiting on me. I'd better hurry on."

Colt wanted to reach for her hand and keep her

there beside him a few more moments. But he didn't have that right. And she'd probably think he was forward. Frankly, he was beginning to wonder if his brain had gone haywire in the past few minutes. He wasn't feeling like his normal self.

"Maybe we'll run into each other again," he suggested.

"Maybe we will." She gave him a little wave, then took off in a hurried stride. As Colt watched her exit the building, Luke walked up behind him.

"For a man who's supposedly bored with women, you seemed to be enjoying Sophia's company."

Turning on his heel, Colt shot his brother a droll frown. "Why shouldn't I enjoy her? She's nice and very pretty."

"And from what Pru tells me, the woman is single," Luke added slyly. "But I doubt that little fact interests you."

Colt rolled his eyes. "You know, brother, I'm beginning to wonder why I ever thought I wanted to move out here to Arizona to work with you. You're nothing but a pain in the rear."

Laughing, Luke gave Colt's shoulder an affectionate slap. "I just had to pull your leg a bit. Actually, I'm glad you had a visit with Sophia. She hasn't been here very long, and I figure it will help her feel more at home to make new friends."

"Well, you know me, I'll do my best to spread a bit of Christmas cheer around the ranch."

Luke laughed again. "How about spreading a little work around? Jim has Daisy Mae, the little dun filly, saddled up in the round pen, and she's just waiting for her first ride. I thought you might be the man for the task."

Colt tugged the brim of his black cowboy hat lower onto his forehead. "Me? The temperature hasn't even reached forty yet, and you want me to climb on a filly that's never been ridden? I didn't expect you to be in such a hurry to get rid of your baby brother."

"Oh, come on, now," Luke urged with a taunting grin. "You know you like a challenge."

The challenge of persuading Sophia to go on a date with him was more to Colt's liking than getting his butt busted on the cold, hard ground. However, that twinkle he'd spotted in Sophia's warm brown eyes told him she'd likely be more of a danger to him than the unbroken filly.

Buttoning his denim jacket up to his throat, Colt motioned for Luke to follow him to the training pen.

"You're right, Luke. I'm just the man for the task."

But as for asking Sophia for a date, he wasn't so sure. For the past several months, he'd purposely avoided women and dates, and the messy entanglements that went along with them. And he'd been a happier guy for sticking to that decision.

Still, Sophia might just be the woman who could

change his mind about dating again. And that was all the more reason he'd be wise to steer clear of her and the temptation.

Chapter Two

When Sophia entered the back door of the kitchen, bright sunshine streamed through the windows and helped to warm the room to a cozy temperature. Across the wide expanse of tiled floor, her grandmother was standing at the industrial-sized stove that boasted eight burners and a large griddle. As she stirred a pot of simmering beef, she looked over her shoulder just in time to see Sophia slipping out of her coat.

"Looks like you came back from the barn empty-handed," she said. "The men must have been hungry."

Even at seventy-four, Reeva stood tall, slim and straight. The long braid that hung down her back was a mixture of black and silver, and though her face was somewhat wrinkled, it was still pretty with high cheekbones and brown eyes that were as sharp and bright as her mind. She'd come to work for the Hollisters as a young woman and she'd stayed because she considered them her extended family. And though Maureen had often tried to get her to slow down and accept more help in the kitchen, Reeva had always refused. Until Sophia had agreed to take the job of assistant cook.

Sophia loved her grandmother more than anyone in the world, and to be working at her side was worth more than any high salary or accolades she might have received if she'd remained an interior designer back in Los Angeles and continued to work her way upward.

After hanging her earmuffs and jacket on a coatrack by the door, she joined Reeva at the stove. "They didn't eat everything. I left what was in the box in Holt's office."

Reeva nodded. "That's good. We won't have to find a place to store it. And the shelves in the pantry are already running over."

Sophia sniffed the air. "I smell pie baking. I wasn't aware that anything special was planned for tonight."

"Nothing special. Maureen wanted mincemeat pie to go with the carne guisada. But she did bring in a few dozen tins to fill with cookies and candy. In the next day or two, she wants those delivered to a couple of nursing homes in town. I think you'd better take inventory. I'm not sure we have enough flour or sugar for that many cookies and candies. You might have to make a trip to the grocery store."

"Wow, it's no wonder the Hollisters decided they needed to hire more help for you in the kitchen. It's a huge job just cooking for the eleven family members who live here in the house. Not to mention the ones who live away from the ranch but often drop in for dinner," Sophia remarked.

"Holidays and special events are celebrated in grand fashion around here. Which means all kinds of extra food has to be prepared," Reeva said as she placed a lid on the cast-iron pot. "There are probably only a handful of days each month when we won't be swamped with extra work. Maureen has been harping for years to bring in another cook to help me. But I never wanted anyone else in my kitchen—getting underfoot and messing up my meals."

"Well, you agreed to let Maureen hire me."

"That's because I trust you to follow my orders," Reeva replied.

Sophia tried not to laugh. "Honestly, I don't know how you've kept this pace for all these years, Gran."

"Well, it was a big help for me when Jazelle came to work a few years ago. She's always been good about helping in the kitchen. Not with the cooking, but with the cleaning up and that sort of thing.

But these days she hardly has time to draw a good breath."

Sophia nodded in agreement. "With all the Hollister siblings married and having babies, Jazelle has turned into more of a nanny than a housekeeper. Just chasing after Blake and Kat's twins is a major job. Andy and Abby never wear down. Not to mention Chandler's two little ones. Evelyn is a sweetheart, but brother Billy is a rascal."

The image of the children put a faint smile on Sophia's face. The children were often loud and rowdy, but they were all adorable. Each time she was near them, her heart ached just a little for the dreams she'd lost. But that sad episode in her life was in the past, she continued to remind herself. And someday, when she met the right man, she would have a husband and children.

"Don't forget. Jazelle has a seven-year-old son and a baby daughter of her own to watch over, too," Reeva said as she walked over to a pair of double ovens and peered through the glass windows. "Maureen is planning to hire a nanny to look after the young ones who live here in the ranch house. But that won't be easy. It takes a special person to care for children in the right way."

"Well, I'm glad she was willing to hire me so quickly," Sophia said. "But I guess it helped that they already knew me."

Reeva turned away from the ovens and walked

over to where a coffee carafe sat on a burner. As she pulled a cup from the cabinet, she darted a concerned look at Sophia. "Honey, every time I look at you I have to pinch myself that you're really here. And then I wonder and worry that you won't stay long."

Groaning, Sophia watched her grandmother fill the cup and stir in a dollop of heavy cream. "Oh, Gran, I don't want you to worry or wonder. There's no need. I'm here to stay. Truly. Surely, you don't think I'll be like Mom? I'm not that kind of person. I took after you. Haven't you figured that out by now?"

Reeva gave her a wry smile. "I have. Except sometimes… Well, it's been a long, long time since I've had family with me. I guess I get to thinking that having you here is too good to last. And then I get to thinking I was wrong in letting you come here. You gave up so much back in California."

Sophia's heart winced as she thought of all the pain and loss her grandmother had gone through over the years. First she'd lost her young husband more than fifty years ago to the Vietnam War. A widow with a baby daughter, she'd used her husband's death benefit and the money she made as a cook to give Liz, Sophia's mother, a decent home and education. But Liz had never appreciated all that her mother had done for her. Liz had never really appreciated anything, except acquiring money and social status. At the age of eighteen she'd left Arizona and practically forgotten that she had a mother.

Sophia went over to her grandmother and curved an arm around the back of Reeva's slim waist. "Gran, please hush. I haven't given up anything. I've gained so much. For the first time in my life I'm doing what *I* want to do. Not what someone else thinks I should do. It's wonderful."

Sniffing, Reeva took a sip from her cup. "I expect Liz hates me even more now that you've moved in with me. She never did want anyone knowing I was a cook on a ranch. That was too degrading for her taste. Now her daughter has followed the same path. I expect your move has put Liz on the verge of having a mental breakdown."

"She's unhappy," Sophia admitted. Which was a wild understatement. Liz had tried every bribe and threat she could think of to keep Sophia in California. But Sophia wasn't going to recount all that ugliness to Reeva. It was not only hurtful, it was pointless. "But she'll get over it. Although she'll probably never admit to her friends that I left for Arizona to be a cook. Frankly, that's her problem, not mine."

Reeva snorted as though to say she doubted Liz would ever come around to her daughter's way of thinking.

"You know, when Maureen's youngest daughter, Camille, went to work as a cook down in Dragoon, everyone thought she'd made a huge mistake," Reeva said. "But it turned out to be *her* thing. Now Camille not only cooks but she owns the whole diner, and she couldn't be happier. Guess I need to remember that."

"Right. This kitchen and living here on the ranch are *my* things, and I'm happy. So quit worrying." Sophia walked over to the end of a long cabinet and tied a white bib apron over her thin black sweater and jeans. "By the way, I met a nice cowboy at the horse barn. We had a cup of coffee together."

"Coffee? I don't recall you taking a thermos of coffee with you."

"The coffee was in Holt's office. From the thermos Jazelle took down there earlier this morning."

Reeva walked over to where Sophia had begun washing the pots and pans used for making the pies.

"Who was this cowboy?"

The suspicious note in Reeva's voice had Sophia grinning at her grandmother. "Colt Crawford. He manages the horse barn. He's Luke Crawford's younger brother."

Reeva looked relieved, and Sophia wondered if her grandmother had been thinking she'd suddenly struck up a conversation with a no-good drifter. But from what Sophia had already learned about Three Rivers, the Hollisters didn't allow that sort of person to work on the ranch.

"I recall Colt. He seems like a nice young man."

"I thought so," Sophia agreed.

"And as good-looking as his brother," Reeva added cleverly.

Sophia smiled playfully at her. "I tried not to notice."

Reeva snorted again. "How did you do that? Drink your coffee with your eyes shut?"

Sophia laughed. "Gran, you're so funny."

Reeva grimaced. "I was young like you once. I know how it feels to look at a strong young man and wonder how it would feel to have his arms around me."

Sophia gasped. "When I looked at Colt I wasn't thinking things like that! Uh...well, I was sort of thinking how cute he was. And I confess I was wondering if he had a girlfriend."

"Well, did you ask him?"

Amazed by her grandmother's response, she stared at her. "Gran! That would have been pushy and forward!"

"Ha! I thought young women nowadays took the bull by the horns. That looking brazen was nothing to worry about."

"Maybe some women have that attitude. But I suppose I'm behind the times. Anyway, I didn't want to give Colt the impression that I was interested."

"Why not? You are, aren't you?"

Shaking her head, Sophia turned back to the sink full of sudsy water. "I don't think I should be interested in Colt or any man right now. I can't think about romance—not yet."

Reeva returned to the stove and gave the simmering meat a few more stirs. "So why were you wondering if Colt has a girlfriend?"

"Oh, curiosity, I suppose."

Quit lying to yourself, Sophia. You thought Colt was good-looking. You kept thinking how nice it might be to spend more time with him. Even if you can't admit that to your grandmother, you should face the fact yourself.

Sophia was trying to mute the voice in her head when Reeva said, "Well, I know for a fact that Colt isn't married. I heard Maureen say that much. But for all I know he might have a dozen girlfriends. 'Course, with him only being here for a few short months, that's highly unlikely. Unless he's a fast worker."

He'd not wasted any time talking her into having coffee with him, Sophia thought. And she'd gotten the impression that he was the type of guy who was very comfortable around the opposite sex. But that hardly mattered to her. Like she'd told her grandmother, she wasn't ready to let herself get close to another man. She was still trying to get over her broken engagement and the betrayal of a man who'd only loved himself.

"Doesn't matter whether Colt is as free as a bird," Sophia said flatly. "It would take a Christmas miracle for me to become his girlfriend."

Reeva chuckled. "Watch out now, honey. Miracles are what Christmas is all about. And it's coming soon."

* * *

Later that night Colt was walking to his truck to make the short drive to the Bar X where he'd rented a house from Joseph and Tessa Hollister. But at the last minute, he changed course and directed his steps toward the bunkhouse. There was nothing at home waiting for him, and at the end of the day, he enjoyed jawing with the men.

The temperature had dropped substantially since the sun had gone down, and the cold wind wasn't helping the stiffness that had been steadily creeping into his body throughout the day. His steps were carefully measured as he entered through the heavy door of the bunkhouse.

The men were already sitting around a long pine table, eating a supper of fried ham and eggs with biscuits fresh out of the oven. The aroma of the just-cooked food caused Colt's empty stomach to growl with hunger.

"Hey, Colt, you're just in time," a cowboy by the name of Leo called out to him. "Grab a plate and fork and join us. There's plenty to go around."

"I'm not sure Colt can make it over here to the table." Riggs winked at Leo, then looked at Colt. "You're walking mighty stiff. Are you sure you don't need for one of us to drive you into town to see a doctor?"

In spite of the soreness and pain in his back, Colt managed to chuckle. "No, thanks. Once I get home a hot shower should fix me."

"What happened? You hit the dirt?"

The question came from Farley, one of the young hands who mostly toted and fetched for the grooms. He had a shock of red hair and a wide, toothy grin. The cowboy was one of the first workers Colt had met when he'd arrived on Three Rivers, and he'd taken an instant liking to the hardworking guy.

"No, Farley. I didn't hit the dirt, but I came close," Colt said as he made his way over to the cabinet to help himself to a plate and silverware.

"Colt rode Daisy Mae, the dun filly that Luke's been working with," Jim explained to the dozen men who were sitting on benches that lined both sides of the pine table. "She bucked like a Texas tornado. I thought for sure she'd toss him, but Colt stuck on her like glue."

"I should have jumped off and saved myself," Colt joked as he piled food on the plate. "I think she jerked my spine into three different pieces. And I'll bet my butt is black and blue."

All the cowboys laughed, except for Farley and Riggs. They were both eyeing Colt as though he needed to be carted off to the nearest hospital.

"Well, you rode her to a standstill, anyway," Jim said. "I'll betcha she won't try that anymore."

"Why didn't Luke or Holt ride her?" one of the men asked. "They're the trainers."

"Colt is a trainer, too," Jim reminded the other

man. "His main job just happens to be barn manager."

Colt sank into an empty space at the end of the bench and began to douse the food on his plate with black pepper. "Right now I don't feel like a manager. More like a hay hauler who's just stacked a few tons in the barn loft."

"Speaking of hay," Leo spoke up, "Blake says two semi-truckloads of alfalfa will be arriving tomorrow. He wants all of it put in the second hay barn. Not sure we have enough room there. Unless we pack more in the loft."

Riggs groaned, and for the next few minutes the men discussed the hay and how to deal with it. Colt was content to eat and simply listen to their chatter. That is, until the subject changed and he heard Sophia's name brought up. All day he'd had trouble keeping his thoughts off the little Christmas angel, and obviously he wasn't the only man who'd been daydreaming about her.

Down the table, he heard the last part of Riggs's sentence.

"…finished my cookies this morning," he said. "I hope she brings more tomorrow."

"I didn't know the Hollisters had hired another girl," Farley commented. "She sure is pretty. I wonder if she has a boyfriend?"

Riggs laughed at the young man's question. "Farley, you can't be as goofy as you look. Sure, she has a boyfriend. A young woman like her can do her picking and choosing. I doubt she'd ever look at a poor cowboy like you."

"I never said she would," Farley shot back at him. "Besides, I have a girlfriend already. She lives over in Aguila."

Riggs snickered and elbowed Jim in the ribs. "So when are we going to see this girl? If there is one."

"There is one, all right!" Farley muttered. "Her hair is the color of corn silk, and her name is Juliann."

The men continued to rib Farley, until Jim cast a speculative look down the table at Colt.

"You guys must've been too busy working to have noticed Colt's already staked a claim on Sophia. She was smiling at him like he was the sun and moon all rolled into one."

"Hell, Colt," Riggs spoke up. "Can't you give us guys a chance once in a while?"

He understood the men were simply having a bit of fun. Still, the idea of them discussing Sophia, even in a joking manner, didn't sit well with him.

"Being polite to a woman is hardly staking a claim," he said.

Jim cleared his throat. "Sorry, Colt. I might've been seeing things wrong. She might've been trying to stake a claim on you."

Colt shot him a droll look. "You need glasses, Jim."

As the men chuckled, Colt wanted to slap his hand on the table and curse. But he tamped down the urge. He was still in the process of getting to know these men and trying to build a good rapport with them. The last thing Colt wanted was to give them the impression he was a stuffed shirt who couldn't take a bit of teasing.

Damn it! What was wrong with him, anyway? Riggs was right. Sophia was the kind of woman who could have her pick of men. For him to be forming possessive ideas about her was downright stupid. If he had any sense at all, he'd think of Sophia as a friend and nothing more.

With that determined thought, Colt quickly finished his meal, then carried the dirty plate and silverware over to the sink where the bunkhouse cook was already busy washing dishes.

"Thanks for the supper, Lester," Colt told the cook, then lifting a hand to the men at the table, started toward the door. "See you guys tomorrow."

Jim called to him. "You leaving already, Colt? Why not stay and play a few hands of poker? In case you're worried about losing, we'll use matches for money."

"No, thanks. I need to get home."

"And take care of his back," Farley said with deadpan seriousness. "If he's too stove-up to work tomorrow, one of us will have to ride that dun filly for him."

"Farley, you have a lot to learn," Jim told him. "Not one of us at this table could ride her and live to tell it."

As Colt stepped outside, he could hear the men roar with laughter. The sound put a faint smile on his face, but it disappeared as he gazed across a maze of holding pens filled with cattle and on to where the three-story ranch house sat nestled among a few giant cottonwoods. Lights were shining through the windows on every floor, and at this time of the evening he figured everyone was getting ready to gather in the downstairs dining room for dinner. A dinner prepared by Sophia and Reeva.

Since her visit to the horse barn this morning, Colt had thought plenty about their short conversation and the bits of information she'd revealed about herself. And he was still musing over the fact that a woman who'd been working as an interior designer had chosen to move to a remote ranch and take a job as a cook. Simply to be with her grandmother?

Colt couldn't swallow that reason. Sure, she probably loved her grandmother. But most women wouldn't give up a lucrative career just to spend her days in a kitchen with one.

No, he'd bet a month's wages that Sophia had run from an unpleasant situation, and it probably involved a man. Most likely, she'd come here to lick her wounds and give her heart a chance to heal. And once that occurred, she'd disappear as quickly as a drop of rain in the desert.

With that sobering thought in mind, he slowly climbed into his truck and headed toward home. Yet as he passed the ranch house, he couldn't help but wonder if Sophia had given him a second thought today. Or had she already forgotten all about him?

Sophia spent the next morning getting ready to make a trip into Wickenburg to pick up supplies when Blake, the general manager of Three Rivers, called the kitchen. He needed to order food for some cattle buyers who'd be visiting his office at noon.

With Reeva busy making homemade tortillas, Sophia had hurriedly put together a mound of sliders stuffed with smoked beef brisket and added a few freshly baked cinnamon rolls for something sweet.

After packing it all in an insulated carrier, she called to Reeva as she headed out the door. "I'm off to Blake's office, Gran. I'll see you when I get back from town. And if you think of anything else we might need from the grocery store, call me."

"Do you have the grocery list?"

Sophia patted the handbag dangling at her side. "Right here. And don't worry. I've gotten the hang of driving a truck. It's the same as a car, only it's higher off the ground and two or three times longer."

The road leading into Three Rivers consisted of more than ten miles of dirt and gravel. A car could travel it, but after a few trips, the rough terrain would soon turn it into a rattling piece of junk. Because only pickup trucks were used for transportation on the ranch, Sophia had had to quickly get accustomed to driving one. At first she'd felt as though she was trying to maneuver a bus. Especially when she'd been attempting to park the vehicle in a slot on the street. But now she was beginning to feel so comfortable in a sturdy truck that she doubted she'd ever want to drive a car again.

Reeva said, "Just remember that you can't drive on dirt like it's the LA freeway."

Sophia chuckled. "Gran, if anyone didn't know, they'd get the idea that you love me."

Trying not to smile, Reeva waved her out the door. "Get out of here and get going. You're wasting daylight, and I don't want to stay up half the night making candy."

Sophia waved over her shoulder at her grandmother before hurrying out the back door of the kitchen.

Moments later, she braked the truck to a stop not far from the entrance of Blake's office, which was situated at one end of a large white cattle barn.

She was standing at the back door of the truck, about to lift the food carrier from the floorboard when she heard a voice call her name.

Glancing around, she spotted Colt riding a bay horse. The man was bundled in a denim jacket lined with warm sherpa, and beneath his black hat she could see his face was reddened from the wind. The mere sight of him was enough to jump her heart into a faster gear.

Postponing her plan to unload the food, she shut the door of the truck and walked over to where he'd reined the horse to a stop near a wooden corral. Sophia noticed how the breaths from the animal's nostrils were creating twin vapor trails in the cold morning air. She also noticed how perfectly at ease Colt looked in the saddle.

"Good morning," she greeted. "Looks like you're hard at work."

He grinned at her, and Sophia was reminded of how those white teeth had gleamed at her yesterday and how bowled over she'd been by his smile.

"I'd be ashamed to call this work. This is fun." He stepped down from the saddle and, holding onto the split reins, led the horse across the short distance to where she was standing. "Holt is behind on his riding, so he asked me to help this morning. I was only too glad to oblige. Most of the guys are hanging Christmas decorations in the barn."

She aimed a censuring look at him. "What are you? A bah-humbug?"

He laughed, and Sophia was instantly lured to the sound and the pleasure on his handsome face. There didn't appear to be anything fake or half-hearted about the man, she decided, and that genuineness drew her to him just that much more.

"Not at all. I'm a ho-ho-ho-I-love-Christmas kind of guy. But if you have a choice of riding a horse or nailing up tinsel and evergreen—well, the horse wins out," he admitted, then arched a questioning brow at her. "What are you up to this morning? Bringing more treats to the cattle barn?"

His dark eyes were a shade shy of black, and at the moment they were making a lazy inspection of her face. The touch of his gaze was almost like being kissed, and the more he looked, the more she could feel her cheeks turning a warm pink. With any luck, he'd think the color was caused from the cold wind.

She shook her head. "No. Blake is expecting cattle buyers later today. I'm delivering food to offer to them."

"Hmm. Normally December is a good time to buy cattle. Prices are low in the winter." He paused and chuckled. "I can save them some time and tell them Blake won't have a low price."

She shot him a pointed smile. "I think Blake would appreciate it if you'd let him do the telling."

He laughed. "Right. He's the big boss. I'd better keep my mouth shut."

"Somehow I find that's a real struggle for you."

Another laugh slipped out of him. "Luke always did tell me that my mouth was my biggest enemy."

She could've told him she liked that he was a

talker. Tristen, her ex-fiancé, had been the silent type and would go for long stretches without speaking. At first she'd thought it made him look like a deep, intelligent thinker and she'd not pressed him to speak. Later on she'd decided his silence made him look more like a moody ass and she'd not cared whether he'd talked or not.

She said, "I'm sure you rarely put your foot in your mouth."

His smile turned soft, and Sophia's heart beat just a tad faster.

"You're being kind."

He and the horse stepped closer, and Sophia realized she needed to mentally slap herself out of the trance she'd fallen into the moment he'd walked up to her. She needed to give him a quick goodbye and get on with her work. But, oh my, he was such a balm to her scarred ego that she didn't want to give up his company.

"Not really," she said.

He patted the horse's neck. "I, uh, have to get back to work. But before I go, I thought I'd ask if you'd do me a little favor."

"I know. You want me to bring more Christmas treats to the horse barn," she said impishly. "Maybe later. Right now Maureen has us on overload making things for charity."

"More cookies at the horse barn would be nice. But the favor I need is more personal. I need advice, and I thought you'd be the perfect person to give it to me," he said. "I'm going to town tomorrow after work to do a bit of Christmas shopping, and I thought you might come along and help me pick out a few gifts. Where my sister-in-law is concerned, I'm at a loss."

Go shopping with him? Did he mean it as a date? Or just two friends going out together? She had to believe the latter. They'd only met yesterday. He couldn't already be thinking of making a date with her.

Why not, Sophia? You'd not been with Colt more than five minutes before you started wondering how it would be to kiss him! Is time really a factor here?

Ignoring the taunting little voice in her head, she said, "Actually, I love to Christmas shop. But I'm not sure when I'll be able to get away from the kitchen tomorrow night. If you wait around on me, all the stores might be closed before we get to town."

The smile on his face said he was hardly worried about time.

"No problem," he said. "I expect most of the stores are having extended holiday hours now. And I won't be leaving the barn early, anyway. Would you like to go?"

Everything inside her was jumping up and down and yelling yes, yes, yes! But she managed to curb all the excitement and give him a demure smile. "It sounds nice, Colt. I would like to go. I can call the horse barn tomorrow afternoon and let you know what time I think I'll be getting off work."

Shaking his head, he quickly pulled a cell phone from his shirt pocket. "Better than that. Just send me a text. Do you have your phone with you?"

"I'll get it from the truck," she told him.

After she'd fetched her phone, they exchanged numbers, and he climbed back aboard the horse he was riding.

"Thanks, Sophia. See you tomorrow evening." He tipped the brim of his hat to her, then trotted the horse off in the opposite direction.

As she watched him go, Sophia let out a sigh that sounded hopelessly besotted. But as she marched over to the truck to collect the food, she told herself it wasn't a wistful sigh at all. It was a what-the-heck-was-she-thinking sigh.

It wouldn't take long for a man like Colt to have a woman so mixed up she wouldn't know her head from her feet. She had no business agreeing to go with him anywhere. It wasn't safe for her peace of mind. But a year and half had passed since she'd thrown her engagement ring in Tristen's face, and since then she'd been playing it safe. She'd been shunning any and every kind of male attention. What was she going to do? Hide forever because she was afraid?

No. She was tired of being afraid and only half living. Besides, Colt hadn't asked her on a serious date. They were going Christmas shopping together. And she darned well intended to enjoy every minute of her time with him.

Chapter Three

It was a quarter after six and already long past dark when Colt walked up to the back of the ranch house and knocked on the kitchen door.

As he waited for someone to answer, he glanced around at the large covered patio that stretched across most of the backyard. On some evenings, the Hollisters had a fire going in the huge firepit where they congregated for drinks and conversation. On a few occasions Colt had joined them, but on most evenings he was too tired to do more than climb in his truck and drive home.

Strange how fresh and energetic he felt tonight. Even with a sore back and bruised buttocks.

The sound of the door opening had him glancing around just in time to see Sophia standing on the threshold. She was dressed casually in jeans and an olive-green button-down shirt, while her long black hair was pulled back from her face with a pair of glittery barrettes. She looked allover pretty, yet it was the bright smile on her face that was making him feel like Christmas had just arrived.

"Hi, Colt."

"Hello, Sophia. Am I too early?"

"Not at all. I'm ready. All I need to do is fetch my coat and handbag." She pushed the door wide and gestured for him to enter. "Come on in. I'll just be a minute."

He stepped past her and into the house. "If your grandmother is still here I'd like to say hello to her," he said.

"She's here. We just finished with the cooking. Jazelle is going to do most of the cleaning up so that I can leave early." She proceeded to lead him through a mudroom and into the long kitchen. "I'm going to have to make it up to her by doing some of her chores, and trust me, she has too many."

Reeva was standing near the stacked double ovens, loading a long glass dish of enchiladas onto a rolling cart. The sound of Colt's and Sophia's approaching footsteps apparently startled her. She slapped a hand to her chest and whirled around to face them.

"Oh, you two slipped up on me!" Her attention went straight to Colt, and she regarded him with a keen eye. "Hello, young man. It's nice to see you again."

Smiling, Colt reached for the older woman's hand and held it warmly between his. "I imagine it's more of a pleasure for me than you," he said. "You're looking fine this evening."

She winked at him. "You know you better be saying that. And in case you're wondering, I'm glad you're taking my granddaughter to town. If she doesn't start getting out and seeing a little excitement, she's going to turn into a wallflower."

Groaning with embarrassment, Sophia said, "This ranch has more than enough excitement for me, Gran."

"Well, I'm happy Sophia agreed to go," Colt told Reeva. "Picking out Christmas gifts is harder for me than wrangling a wild horse, so I'm going to ask her to do all the choosing."

Colt couldn't help but notice that Sophia was carefully watching the exchange between him and her grandmother. Perhaps she hadn't expected him to be so friendly with Reeva. Or it could be that Sophia thought he was simply being nice to Reeva to earn Brownie points with her and her grandmother. If so, she'd be wrong on both counts. In truth, the very first time he'd met Reeva she'd reminded him of his own grandmother that he'd lost a few years ago, and he'd immediately felt a connection to her.

"We'd better be going before all the stores close," Sophia spoke up. "I'll get my coat and handbag."

While Sophia moved away to collect her things, Colt patted the back of Reeva's hand and her fingers tightened around his. The gesture of trust touched Colt in a very unexpected way. "Don't worry, Reeva, I'll take care and make sure your granddaughter gets home at a decent hour."

Reeva gave him another wink, then said in a hushed tone, "Just make sure you don't have her home too early."

Colt gave her a conspiring grin. "I'll make sure that doesn't happen."

"Make sure what doesn't happen?" Sophia asked.

He turned to see she was standing a few steps behind him. A green plaid coat and brown leather handbag were draped over her arm.

"Oh, I was just reassuring your grandmother that we won't skip supper." Colt quickly took the coat from her and helped her into the garment. "Reeva says you're tired of eating her cooking."

Sophia playfully rolled her eyes. "I don't believe a word either one of you are saying."

Chuckling, Colt bade Reeva good-night, then led Sophia out of the kitchen.

As they walked the short distance to the gate that opened to a small parking area, Colt gestured to the sky. "Look at all those stars. Did you ever see anything like that in Los Angeles?"

She paused to gaze up at the sky. "If I could manage to see through the smog and artificial lights. Otherwise, to really see the sky, I'd have to travel to the outskirts of the city. But this sky over Three Rivers is usually a stunning sight. Like tonight."

He urged her forward. "Too bad Santa isn't flying his sleigh tonight. Rudolph would have a clear flight path with all these stars lighting up the sky."

Amused, she glanced at him. "So you're really into Christmas?"

Pausing, he turned to face her. "Well, sure. There's so much magic in Christmas. The wonder. And having faith. Even in things that we can't see."

His remark appeared to surprise her.

"That's nice. I wish…" She seemed to be thinking deeply.

"Go on," he urged. "You wish…?"

Shaking her head, she looked beyond him and into the darkness. "Nothing. We're grown adults, and it's a childish wish."

"God help us if we ever lose sight of the child inside of us. Kids are often more perceptive about things than grown-ups."

Shrugging, she focused her gaze back on his face. "I was only going to say that I wish I'd been taught about the wonder and faith of Christmas. My mother was, and still is, all about the gifts. The money spent. That sort of thing."

"It's never too late to learn, Sophia. Living here on the ranch—you're going to see how different things can be. And I don't mean in terms of city versus country. I'm talking about people now."

A faint smile touched her lips. "I'm already seeing that."

Was she? Colt could only wonder what she was really thinking about the drastic changes she'd recently made. Once the novelty of ranching life wore off, she might realize she'd given up too much by leaving Los Angeles.

As they strolled on through the yard gate and across the graveled parking area, he said, "Believe it or not, I've been close to your hometown."

By now they'd reached the passenger door of his black truck, and as he opened the door, she looked at him.

"I'm surprised. What were you doing in California?"

"Attending the Los Alamitos Equine Sale. It's an annual event where quarter horse racing stock is sold. I went with my old boss."

"Did you purchase any horses?"

"He did. Five to be exact. We had hell—uh, sorry—we had heck getting them back to Clovis. After three blown tires and two horses refusing to drink and eventually having colic, we finally made it home a week later than planned."

"Sounds like an unforgettable trip," she said dryly.

Chuckling, he said, "Oh, it was like anything else. Once you get over the pain, you mostly remember the good."

"That's a nice way of thinking," she murmured.

Her gaze settled on his face, and Colt found himself studying the plush line of her dusky pink lips. He'd kissed plenty of girls in his lifetime, but something told him that kissing Sophia would be different. Not because she was nicer, or prettier, or even sexier. No, it would be different just because it was her.

"It's the only way of thinking," he told her.

He cupped a hand around her elbow to assist her climb into the cab. After she was settled, he walked around and slid into the driver's seat. As he put the truck into gear and pulled away from the house, he noticed she was gazing with interest at the interior.

"Your truck is very nice," she said.

He glanced over to find she was looking at him, and he consciously swiped a hand over his chin. "Sorry I didn't have time to shave. We had more than usual going on at the barn today. Jim, one of the grooms, stayed on to see that things were wrapped up so that I could leave early. I'm going to owe him a favor like you owe Jazelle."

"The whiskers don't bother me. Besides, I hardly look like I've stepped out of the hair salon." She snapped her seat belt in place and crossed her legs. "One of the things I love about my job on Three Rivers is the people working with me. No one is worried about having to do more than the other person. And everyone is willing to help when and where they're needed."

He said, "I think that's because the Hollisters have set standards, and they hire people that are only too happy to live up to those standards."

"You're probably right." She turned slightly toward him. "How did you come about hiring on with Three Rivers Ranch? Was it something you'd been trying for and an opening came up?"

"Not exactly. I guess you could say I was fairly happy with the T Bar T where I worked in New Mexico. The operation wasn't anything close to the size of Three Rivers, but it was good-sized, and the owners were fair people. There was never enough help to cover all the work, though. Still, I didn't have any intentions of leaving. Not until Luke told me they were needing a barn manager and that Holt wanted me. Can you imagine? A guy like Holt Hollister wanting me to work in his horse division? I couldn't. The only thing I can figure is that Luke must have really bragged about me," he added with a little laugh.

"Don't kid yourself. Before anyone is hired, Maureen gets plenty of references and makes a thorough background search. She did that even with me. And she's known me since I was a little girl."

Surprised, he glanced at her. "I didn't realize you went that far back with the family."

"Oh, yes. My grandmother has worked for the Hollisters since she was very young, and she's seventy-four now, so you can do the math."

"Wow. After all those years, Reeva's probably considered a part of the family. What about your grandfather? Is he living?"

"No. He was killed during Vietnam, shortly after he and Gran were married. She was pregnant with my mother when she lost him."

"That's tragic. So obviously you never knew him."

"No. And Gran never remarried. She raised my mother alone—doing all sorts of manual jobs until she took the job as cook here on Three Rivers. I've always admired her enormously for being so strong and independent. Some people break under the kind of weight she was handed, but not Gran."

"No one had told me that Reeva was a widow. Not that being a widow is unusual, but remaining one for all those years isn't typical."

Her sigh was so soft that Colt barely picked up the wistful sound.

"You were talking about the Hollister standards a minute ago. Well, I think the same thing goes for Gran. She never found another man that could measure up to her late husband."

Sophia's observation had Colt's thoughts turning to his own parents. His father, Mills, had never remarried after his wife, Paula, had died. Maybe that was because he'd never found anyone he could love the way he'd loved her. But as far as finding another woman who could live up to her standards? No, that would be highly unlikely. She'd been a beautiful woman, and she'd also been bipolar. Because of her condition, she'd given her husband and children reason for plenty of concern. But Colt had always tried to focus on the pleasant memories of his mother. For the most part, she'd been charming and loving. And though she'd been a paradox, he still missed her.

"You're probably right about that." He cast a questioning glance at her. "Do you hear from your mother often?"

Her lips twisted. "Unfortunately, my phone is inundated with messages from her."

Colt was hesitant to ask why, but she'd thrown the tidbit out there. He'd look damned indifferent if he didn't say something.

"I'm assuming you don't approve of getting all those messages." He flashed her a grin. "What is she? A controlling mother?"

Her answer was a laugh that sounded like something between a groan and a sob.

"Oh, Colt. If you weren't driving, I think I'd kiss you."

The unexpected remark caused his foot to ease on the accelerator. "Uh…should I pull over and stop the truck?"

This time her laugh was genuine. "No. But I do appreciate you understanding the situation without asking me a bunch of stupid questions."

"Remember me telling you about my mouth? Trust me, Sophia, I can ask stupid questions. But listen, you don't have to tell me anything about your mother. We're on a Christmas-shopping trip. We're not headed to a psychiatrist's office."

She flashed him a wide smile. "Has anyone ever told you that you're sort of funny? In a sweet way?"

He pretended to think about that for a moment. "*Funny* and *sweet*? No. Usually adjectives like *goofy* and *frustrating* are thrown at me."

"I seriously doubt that," she said, then let out a long sigh. "Anyway, I do need to explain a bit about Mom. Otherwise, you'll think I'm a disrespectful daughter. And that's not really the case. She has issues that… Well, she hasn't seen or spoken to her own mother in years."

Colt didn't bother to hide his surprise. "She hasn't spoken to Reeva? Is this a joke?"

"I wish it was a joke. But it isn't," she said soberly.

Colt had known people who'd been estranged from a relative or close friend. The situations were always ugly and usually senseless. But try as he might, he couldn't imagine anyone having such a long-term riff with Reeva. She was a decent, hardworking person. What could she have done to deserve her daughter's desertion?

"That's damned unfortunate."

He wanted to ask more, but from the corner of his eye, he could see she was staring morosely at the dark landscape in front of them. And he didn't want to get the evening off to a bad start by prying into such a personal subject.

"It's sad and frustrating," she said. "When I grew old enough to learn there was such a thing as a grandmother, I wanted to know mine. Mom refused. At that time I was just a little girl. Too little to travel here to Arizona alone to meet her."

"What happened? How did you finally contact your grandmother?"

She slanted him a wry smile. "You said that kids are perceptive. Well, they're ingenious, also. I secretly dug through some of Mom's papers and found Gran's name. From there I acquired her phone number and where she lived. I'll never forget how she sounded that first time I called her. She cried and laughed."

"I can't imagine what Reeva must have thought. Did she know that she had a granddaughter?"

"Yes. At that time Mom still communicated with her on rare occasions. But never made any effort to see her. Mom was, and still is, embarrassed that her mother works as a ranch cook. In fact, she's always told her friends that Reeva worked as a secretary. She doesn't want anyone knowing the truth."

"Wow. That's tough. When did your mother leave Arizona?"

She grimaced. "When she was eighteen. Just old enough to legally be on her own. She hated it here and wanted more from life than what Gran could give her."

"That didn't mean she needed to lie and cut off ties," Colt pointed out.

"When my mom doesn't like someone, she cuts that person out of her life. In her mind, that fixes everything."

Sophia had left a high-paying job to become a cook like her grandmother. The very occupation that embarrassed her mother. Colt mulled that fact over before he finally glanced in her direction. "Is that why you left California and became a cook? Just to spite your mother?"

The look on her face was a mixture of disappointment and disbelief. "Do you honestly believe I'm a spiteful person?"

"No. But I figure other folks might see it that way."

"I don't care about those other folks. No matter what angle you look at it from, spite is a wasteful thing. Moving to Three Rivers was all about what I wanted in my life. And nothing to do with getting back at Mom."

The flat tone in her voice said his suggestion had annoyed her. But heck, she was the one who'd thrown all this information at him, Colt thought. He'd not asked her to expose her family's laundry to him.

"I guess this means you're not feeling the urge to kiss me anymore?"

She looked at him with confusion before she burst out laughing. "Let's just say the urge has passed... for the moment."

He silently repeated those last three dangling words. Did she mean not now, but later—maybe? He quickly answered himself with a mental shake of his head. Sophia's kiss, in any form or fashion, wasn't something he needed to be thinking about. He wasn't ready to start playing dating games again.

What makes you think Sophia would want to play any kind of games with a man? Can't you see that she's family material? She wants commitment. Not a chase around the bedroom.

The mocking voice going on inside his head caused his cheeks to warm and a choking sensation to attack his throat. He attempted to clear it away before he spoke.

"I imagine I'd be right in saying you're saving those kisses for your boyfriend."

"You'd be wrong. I don't have a boyfriend." Beneath a veil of black lashes, she regarded him with a curious glance. "What about you, Colt? Does your girlfriend mind you taking me shopping instead of her?"

Was she actually interested, or just making conversation? He wanted to believe the latter. It was safer that way. "No," he said with a wry grin. "I don't have a girlfriend. I—uh—haven't dated in a long while."

His reply was met with silence and then he heard her let out a long breath that sounded very close to a sigh.

"Then that makes us even," she said. "I haven't dated in a long time, either."

Even though he wanted to ask her why she'd avoided dating, he kept the question to himself. This trip to town was meant to be a friendly outing for the two of them and nothing more. And he needed to make sure it stayed friendly.

Five minutes later they reached Wickenburg, and Sophia wasn't surprised when Colt made his first stop at the largest western store in town.

"You must already have something in mind for gifts," she said as the two of them passed through a glass door and entered the carefully laid-out store of western clothing, footwear, jewelry and riding tack.

"I have something in mind for Luke and little J.J. But Prudence is another matter. Let's go over to the boots."

They headed in the direction of the footwear department. Along the way, they passed a large decorated blue spruce tree and a tiered circle of red and white poinsettia plants. Holiday music was playing over the in-house speakers, while the scents of gingerbread lingered faintly in the air.

The atmosphere was enough to turn Sophia's thoughts back to the remarks Colt had made about Christmas. His childlike faith had endeared her. Particularly when she'd compared his feelings about the holiday to Tristen's. Her ex-fiancé had grumbled about the interruptions in his schedule, the long lines at the stores, the obligation of giving gifts.

No. Tristen hadn't been fun to be with during the holidays. And the more she was around Colt, the more she realized Tristen hadn't been much fun at any time of the year.

Too bad it had taken her so long to figure out that he wasn't the sort of man she wanted to be married to, Sophia thought ruefully. But that was all in the past. She was starting over with a new home and job. And tonight she was out with a man who made her smile. That was enough to make her want to sing a Christmas carol.

"Do you know what style of boots your brother likes?" she asked as he began searching through an assortment of colors and sizes.

"I ought to. I'm usually the one who buys his boots. He'll wear them until holes are worn into the soles before he gets a new pair. Don't get me wrong, he's far from being a tightwad. He's just not a shopper."

He picked up a copper-brown boot. The tops were

smooth leather embroidered with fancy stitching, while the foot was a rough, beautiful texture that Sophia had never seen before.

"I was thinking I might really splurge and get him a pair made of something exotic like these. They're made from a pirarucu fish that lives in the Amazon. Snazzy, huh?"

"Gorgeous," Sophia agreed, "but I'd probably fall over in a faint if I looked at the price tag."

"I don't carry any smelling salts with me so I'll keep the price a secret," Colt joked.

She watched him return the boot to its spot on the shelf. "You're putting them back?"

He nodded. "Now that I give it more thought, Luke doesn't like the idea of endangering a species to make boots and belts and handbags. Neither do I. He'd be happier with plain old bull hide."

"So you two are eco-friendly cowboys," she stated. "Is that unusual?"

"Not at all. The land makes our living. We need the ecosystem to stay balanced. For us and all the animals."

She tossed him a wide smile. "Even flying reindeer, I suppose?"

"Oh, especially flying reindeer."

He crooked a finger for her to come closer to him and the rows of shelved boots. "Show me what you think Luke would like in the way of boots, and I'll tell you whether you passed the test."

She groaned good-naturedly. "Colt, that's not fair. I've only seen him a couple of times."

He chuckled. "Don't worry. You'll still get to eat, even if you don't pass the test."

"Oh, well, that's reassuring," she said with a laugh.

Several minutes later, after Sophia had flunked the boot test, Colt chose a pair made of brown rough-out leather for Luke, but she did help him choose a tiny matching pair for his thirteen-month-old nephew.

As the two of them walked in the direction of the checkout counter, Sophia remarked, "I see there's a large selection of women's things on the opposite side of the store. While we're here do you want to look for a gift for Prudence?"

Pausing, he glanced thoughtfully over at the women's department. "Prudence does wear boots and western clothing. And she is learning to ride. But having a sister-in-law is still new to me. I don't want to give her something that would make her feel awkward. I'd rather let Luke get her something in the way of cowgirl gear. Does that make sense to you?"

Sophia took a moment to weigh his question. "I don't have a sibling or an in-law, but I think you're right about leaving the more personal items to Luke. Getting her something she could use for work should be a safe gift. She's a school superintendent and—"

An idea suddenly struck her and she quickly grabbed his hand. "Come with me."

Moments later, Sophia found a beautifully hand-tooled leather briefcase and held it up for his inspection. "What do you think? To carry her laptop and essentials back and forth to work. It's professional and western at the same time. And it's such a nice piece it will last forever." Tilting her head to one side, she tried to read the expression on his handsome face. "Unless you don't want to spend quite so much."

"Are you kidding? Prudence has made my brother so happy that I could never give her enough." Smiling broadly, he gently patted her cheek. "This is great, Sophia. I knew you'd be perfect at this gift-finding thing."

His praise sent a shot of joy through her, and she laughed softly. "I got lucky, that's all."

He wrapped his hand around her upper arm, and Sophia couldn't ignore the warmth that radiated from his fingers, down through the fabric of her blouse, and all the way to her flesh.

"So did I," he said.

Confused by his remark, she looked up at him. "Lucky that you managed to find three gifts in one store?"

He chuckled lowly. "No. I'm lucky to have you with me tonight."

It would be easier on her peace of mind to think

he was teasing. Yet the twinkle in his dark eyes was serious enough to make her heart beat faster.

Purposely making her voice light and playful, she said, "Before the night is over you might start regretting my company."

He urged her in the direction of the checkout counter. "Don't worry. I'll tell you if you're giving me a headache."

Headache? Heartache? There was little doubt in Sophia's mind that Colt could give her both of those woes. If she let him. But she wasn't going to allow herself to get that close to the cowboy. She didn't want his kisses, she told herself. All she wanted was his friendship.

Chapter Four

After Colt paid for the items and locked them safely in the back floorboard of his truck, he suggested the two of them walk down the sidewalk to a popular café.

"The place isn't fancy," he warned her as they neared the entrance of the green stucco-fronted building, "but the food is tasty. 'Course, it's not as tasty as what you and Reeva prepare."

"Don't worry. I'm not picky," she assured him. "And since I've not taken the time to eat anything since early this morning, I'm running on empty. What about you?"

"I confess I ate one of Holt's pastries this afternoon. But only one."

With a hand against the small of her back, he guided her through the elongated room that reminded Sophia of a diner rather than a café. Red vinyl booths lined one whole wall, while on the opposite side of the room, a long, Formica-topped bar was equipped with swiveling stools covered in the same red vinyl as the booths. At the moment, several people were seated at the bar. Some were only drinking coffee, while others were eating a meal.

At the first vacant booth they came to, Colt helped her out of her coat and onto the bench seat. By the time he'd removed his hat and jacket and slipped into the seat across from her, a young waitress with long pink hair coiled into a ballerina bun arrived to take their order.

As she placed a couple of menus and two glasses of ice water in front of them, Sophia could tell from the slump of her shoulders and the bored look on her face that the woman was merely trying to get through her shift.

"The special tonight is meat loaf. It's not bad," she told them. "And the macaroni and cheese that comes with it is baked, so it's pretty good."

Colt opened the menu and began to study it, but Sophia didn't bother.

"You've sold me," Sophia told the waitress. "I'll take the special."

Colt glanced over at her. "That was quick."

She smiled. "I'm a girl who usually knows what she wants when she sees it."

The waitress must have taken Sophia's comment as suggestive because her brows arched as she glanced in a speculative way at the two of them.

Grinning, Colt handed his menu to the waitress. "I'll take the special, too."

"Good choice," the waitress told him.

After she'd scribbled down their orders and gone on her way, Sophia looked over at Colt. He was studying her with a look that was impossible for her to decipher. But she didn't need to know what he was thinking to recognize he was a guy who could turn a woman's head. Even hers, if she wasn't careful.

She drew in a long breath and released it. "I hope you chose the special because you wanted it and not because I settled for it."

"I like meat loaf and macaroni and cheese. That's why I chose it. And I don't get homestyle cooking all that much. Some evenings I stop by the bunkhouse and eat with the hands. But Lester, the bunkhouse cook, isn't too inventive with his meals. What he does prepare is pretty good, though."

"You don't live with the guys in the bunkhouse?" she asked.

"No. I'm renting a house from Joseph and Tessa. It's on their ranch, the Bar X."

With the Bar X located only a short distance from Three Rivers, Tessa passed the ranch each time she drove to town. Tessa had even invited Sophia to stop by for a visit. It was something she planned to do as soon as she could make time in her busy work schedule.

"What I see of the ranch as I drive by is beautiful," Sophia told him. "From the few conversations I've had with Tessa, I can see how proud she is of the place. Especially because the property was an inheritance from her father. You've probably already been told that he'd been a longtime sheriff of Yavapai County and that Tessa grew up not knowing him. I think… Well, that's a sad thing."

His gaze made a slow perusal of her face. "You say that like you've gone through the same experience. I recall you saying your parents were divorced, but I assumed your dad was still a part of your life."

Sophia hoped the bitterness she was feeling didn't show on her face. She hated the emotion and constantly fought to keep it from having an impact on her hopes and plans. "No. Mom made sure of that. She purposely cut him out of my life."

"Because he wasn't a decent person? Or was she using you for spite?" Before she could answer, he shook his head in a rueful way. "Sorry. I shouldn't have asked that last question. Heck, I wouldn't know your mother if she walked through the door of this café right now. I shouldn't be assuming anything about the woman."

The waitress arrived with their orders of iced tea

and Sophia waited until the young woman had left the table before she replied.

"Your question didn't offend me, Colt. Mom is all about spite and control—especially when it suits her purposes. But I'm not a child anymore, and I can make decisions for myself. Recently, I made an effort to reach out to my father, and we're getting to know each other through phone calls and emails. So all is not lost."

"You're lucky that you have something to salvage," he said.

Sophia suddenly felt like a heel. Here she'd been lamenting about being separated from her father, but Colt would never be able to see or talk with his mother again.

"Yes. Very lucky," she murmured, then purposely changing the subject, asked, "How did you come about living on the Bar X? There wasn't any vacant housing available on Three Rivers?"

He shook his head, and Sophia caught herself gazing at the way the dim overhead light glinted off the black waves of his hair and partially shadowed his rugged features. Since they'd entered the café, she'd noticed several women glancing in his direction. Which was hardly a surprise. Tall, dark and sexy didn't begin to describe Colt's appearance. Just looking at him was downright dangerous.

He said, "Luke moved into the last vacant house on the ranch. And the former barn manager lived in the bunkhouse, so his leaving didn't vacate anything. But it's no big deal. The Bar X is only a few miles from Three Rivers, and I like the little house I'm living in. It's at the back of the bluff that sits behind Joe and Tessa's place. Actually, it's more like a cabin than a house. Tessa explained that her father had it built as a sort of getaway. The view there is spectacular—that is, whenever I have the chance to sit and appreciate it. And since Joe and Tessa only charge me a pittance for rent, I couldn't be happier."

"Sounds nice," she said but stopped short of saying she'd like to see it sometime. No way was she going to be that suggestive. He might get the wrong idea and think she was looking for a casual affair.

"What about you, Sophia? Are you living in the ranch house with the Hollisters?"

"Oh, no. With three families living in the house, that only leaves two guest rooms, and those are needed for visitors. I live with Gran in a small house on another part of the ranch. In fact, the place isn't far from your brother and sister-in-law's house."

"Luke mentioned that Reeva lived down the road from him. But I've never driven any farther than his house. Has she always lived there?"

Sophia nodded. "Axel Hollister, Joel and Gil's father, had the house built especially for Reeva. He didn't want her driving the long distance from town to the ranch. And Gran, being so independent, refused to take up room in the main ranch house, so the Hollisters built her one of her own."

"Do you like living with her?"

She smiled wanly. "Okay, you'll probably think this is corny, but living with Gran is like having the kind of loving mother I never had."

"Doesn't sound a bit corny to me," he said. "So you're planning on staying with her instead of finding a place of your own?"

"For now. The setup works for both of us."

He smiled gently. "Sounds like a good deal for the two of you."

Their food arrived, and as they dug in to the homestyle meal, Sophia could only think how much her life had changed since she'd left Los Angeles three weeks ago. It was like she'd gone from running on a fast treadmill to strolling down a quiet country lane. Naturally, she'd expected the change of pace. But to be out dining with a real-life cowboy? No. She'd not imagined anything of the sort.

"Tell me, Colt, how did you celebrate Christmas when you lived in New Mexico? Did you have holiday traditions?"

"Dad lives fairly close to where Luke and I used to work. We'd both spend Christmas Day with him. With all three of us bachelors… Well, we weren't big on decorating. But Dad always puts up a Christmas tree. Sometimes it might be leaning and the decorations are hanging a little cockeyed. But he puts his heart into it. I kind of feel bad because he's going to be without us boys this year. With foaling season starting up, it's not a good time for me or Luke to be away from the ranch. And Dad hates to travel for any distance. So we've been trying to talk him into inviting a neighbor lady over. She's had a crush on him for years, but he says she gets on his nerves. We'll see."

She smiled while thinking of her own father. He'd told Sophia that he lived with a certain woman for a while now but had never married her. Gauging from the remarks he'd made to Sophia, she got the impression that he considered one attempt at matrimony enough for him. Maybe one attempt at being engaged should be enough for Sophia, she thought. Perhaps if she was truly smart, she'd make herself forget all about finding a husband one day and having children. But how did a woman just throw away her dreams?

Shaking away the dull thoughts, she asked, "What about the ranch where you worked in New Mexico? Were the owners big on celebrations like the Hollisters?"

His wry chuckle spoke volumes. "Not in the least. Oh, they had their parties, but they were all private affairs. None of the T Bar T employees were ever invited. We were there to work as ranch hands and for no other reason. Any socializing that went on among the hands was done when we met in the nearby town."

"Hmm. I guess it would be safe to say the barns on the T Bar T didn't get spruced up with evergreen boughs or red bows like the ones on Three Rivers."

"Not hardly. There wasn't a pretty cook bringing cookies and candy to the barn, either." The amusement on his face disappeared as he added, "To be honest, Sophia, none of us hands on the T Bar T thought there was anything strange about being kept separate from the owners. When Luke began to tell me all about Three Rivers and how the Hollisters did things, I thought he was exaggerating. No ranch could be run as though it was one big happy family."

"Now you're learning differently," Sophia stated the obvious.

"Yes. And I'm still continuously surprised by the Hollisters' generosity." He ate a few bites of meat loaf before he leveled a curious gaze at her. "That's enough about me. Tell me about your Christmases in California. Did you usually spend them with your mother?"

"Always. She usually has friends over for dinner. Which I never minded—the more the merrier. But Mom is the sort who frets over every detail. She has to make certain everything is perfectly planned and carried out on schedule."

"Sounds like a job instead of a celebration."

Shrugging, she said, "In my opinion, it takes all the fun and spontaneity out of the holiday. You talked about your father's Christmas tree not being so perfect. Well, I wish my mom could be more like that. She always has to have everything coordinated or monochrome, and each decoration has to be placed in a certain spot at a precise angle. But thank goodness this year I won't have to deal with any of that. Gran and I are planning to have an old-fashioned tree. And trim it with strings of cranberries and popcorn."

"What about paper chains? Luke and I used to make those out of colored construction paper."

She gave him a bright smile. "That's a great idea, Colt! Now, all Gran and I need is the extra time to make the decorations. And that's going to be hard to find with all the additional cooking we'll be doing for the coming holiday."

"I'll think about you doing all that extra cooking while I'm hooked spending hours in the foaling barn. By the time Christmas arrives, the babies will be coming fast and furious. It's an exciting time but exhausting, too. We have to make sure mother and baby get safely through the births. Most of the time everything goes smoothly, but occasionally things can go wrong. And it's tragic to lose a foal."

To Sophia's horror, tears suddenly stung the back of her eyes, and she quickly swallowed hard and blinked her eyes in an effort to ward them off. Not for anything did she want him to guess the subject of babies and births, even of an equine nature, had caused her to become emotional.

"I'll keep you all in my prayers," she murmured,

then clearing her throat, she glanced over toward the bar. "I wonder if I could get a cup of coffee? I'm feeling a little cold."

"Sure thing." He cast a concerned glance at her before he motioned to the waitress. "I hope you're not getting sick."

Trying not to look embarrassed, she shook her head. "Oh, no, I'm fine." She hoped he wouldn't ask any more questions.

Colt couldn't help but notice that Sophia had grown quiet during their drive back to Three Rivers. Actually, the more he thought about the change in her, the more he decided that something had flipped a switch in her during the last of their meal. She'd talked about being cold, but he'd gotten the feeling there was more to the change in her mood.

Once they'd left the café, they'd made a short stop at a discount store, but she'd been mostly noncommittal as he'd picked up items to wrap the gifts he'd purchased. He'd tried to think of anything he might have said to offend her, but nothing came to mind. Up until now, he'd not thought of Sophia as being a moody person, but he realized he was only beginning to know her. And everyone had their quiet moments from time to time.

"Looks like Luke is still awake," he commented as they passed by his brother's place. "There's a light on in every room. They probably can't get J.J. to go to sleep. Since my little nephew started walking, he can be a real handful."

"Prudence stopped by the ranch house the other evening, and J.J. was with her," she replied. "He's very cute. Your brother must be awfully proud of him."

"Having a son has put Luke over the moon. In fact, he and Prudence are already trying for another baby. She recently turned forty, and she's thinking she doesn't want to wait and possibly miss the chance to have more children."

She looked at him. "And Luke agrees with her plan?"

"Oh, for sure," he said, then flashed her a smile. "I'll be honest, I never pictured my big brother turning into such a family man. For years he swore he'd always be a bachelor. Just goes to show that people can change. Now, he'd love for him and Prudence to have two or three more kids."

"Must be nice," she murmured.

For Luke or Prudence or both of them? She didn't elaborate on her remark, and Colt didn't press her. Instead, he drove on down the narrow dirt road to where he knew Reeva's small house was located. The outside consisted of aqua-colored stucco accented with a dark wooden door and matching trim around the windows. A stand of mesquite trees shaded the front yard, while off to the left was a small chicken house with a connecting yard protected by high wire.

All in all, it was a pretty little home, but he figured it had to be a far cry from what Sophia had left behind in Los Angeles. Although, he didn't know why his thoughts kept comparing Sophia's previous life with the one she had now. None of that had anything to do with Colt.

Except that he wanted her to be happy here.

Damn, what kind of syrupy thought was that? Sophia had to worry about her own happiness. Just like he had to be responsible for his.

"Well, here we are," he said as he braked the truck and shut off the motor. "Looks like Reeva left the porch light on for you. Think she's waiting up to make sure you get home safely?"

She gave a droll look. "I'm twenty-six years old. She's not worried about me. Especially now—" she turned her gaze on the house "—that I-I'm living here with her."

He got the impression she'd been about to say something else but at the last second had decided against it.

He glanced pointedly at his watch. "Well, I promised her that I wouldn't get you home too early. Maybe she'll think I've kept you out long enough."

"You honestly promised Gran such a thing?"

Using his forefinger he crossed his heart. "I did. She thinks you need to have a little fun. But I... I'm getting the feeling that you've not had much of that this evening."

Her lips parted with surprise, and Colt was suddenly struck with the urge to pull her close and discover for himself just how it would feel to have her mouth fastened to his.

"I can't imagine why you'd think such a thing," she told him. "The evening has been very pleasant for me."

He moved his gaze off her lips and up to her wide brown eyes. "Really? You've not talked much since we finished dinner."

"Oh. I hadn't realized. I'm sorry if I seemed distant. It's been a long day, and I've had lots on my mind."

He dared to reach over and take her hand in his. "I was afraid I'd offended you somehow. If I did, it wasn't my intention."

She glanced awkwardly toward the windshield. "That's nonsense. You've been delightful company."

He smiled. "*Delightful*, huh? I don't think anyone has ever used that adjective to describe me. I think I like it."

Her gaze turned back to his face, and the soft smile on her lips had Colt forgetting his plan to remain on a no-woman diet.

"And I like that you can be funny. I like that a whole lot."

He smoothed the tips of his fingers over the back of her hand and part of his brain was registering the softness of her skin while the other part of him wondered what she might do if he did try to kiss her. Slap him? Push him away? No. He didn't want to chance making her angry or disappointed in him. If he ever did get the opportunity to kiss her, he wanted to hear her sigh with longing and feel her arms slip around his neck.

Clearing his throat, he said, "Well, it's getting late. I'll walk you to the door."

After helping her out of the truck, he offered her his arm, and they walked up a narrow walk-way edged with large river rock. The porch was a small square of brown brick with a roof to protect the door. A wrought iron lantern attached to the side of the house shed a golden glow over Sophia's face, and Colt was surprised to see her expression had turned shy.

A tentative smile touched her lips. "Gran was right, you know. I do need to get out more and have a bit of fun. I'd almost forgotten what it was like. Thank you, Colt, for inviting me tonight."

The sincerity in her voice caught him off guard, and for a moment he couldn't come up with a sen-sible reply. Especially when thoughts of pulling her into his arms were consuming every cell in his brain.

"No, you have it backward, Sophia. You made gift buying fun for me." He jabbed his hands in the pock-ets of his jacket to deter the temptation to touch her. "Uh, maybe we can make another go of it—shopping,

I mean. I still have a long list of gifts to buy. What about you?"

"I've not even started yet," she admitted, then smiled at him. "I'll think about going again—on one of my evenings off."

"Same here."

Before he could guess her intentions, she rose up on the tips of her toes and placed a soft kiss on his cheek.

"Good night, Colt. Have a safe drive back to the Bar X."

Before he could gather his senses enough to bid her good-night, she slipped into the house and shut the door behind her.

Colt drew in a deep breath and blew it out before he finally made himself step off the porch and walk back to his truck.

This night hadn't gone anything like he'd planned, and that scared the heck out of him. For the first time in his life, he'd met a woman who hadn't bored him. And if he wasn't careful, he could get to liking Sophia way too much.

His brother would probably tell him that getting involved with Sophia would be a good thing. But Luke was different. He was happily married. He wanted to be a family man. Whereas Colt got a chill just imagining himself as a husband.

Marriage was a serious business. It wasn't something a person should just walk away from if things didn't work. He'd learned that from the deep devotion his father had held for his mother. Yet, Colt hadn't met a woman who'd made him want to commit a lifetime of love to her. No, Colt thought, he was better off steering clear of a serious relationship with Sophia, or any woman.

Colt had planned to spend the next day helping his brother with the yearling training. Instead, he ended up assisting Holt tend to two foaling mares. Thankfully, both mares experienced easy deliveries, and their foals were healthy.

Chandler, who was the second oldest of the Hollister brothers and a revered veterinarian, remained so busy with his animal clinic in town that he was rarely on the ranch during daylight hours. And at nights, barring a dire emergency, Holt refrained from calling his brother to the barn in order to let the man rest.

Fortunately, Colt was knowledgeable with the birthing process. In fact, one of the major reasons Holt had wanted him for the barn-manager position was so he could assist with deliveries during the chaotic foaling season. Meanwhile, Holt had been pushing Blake and his mother to hire a resident veterinarian for the ranch. Not only to help with the horses but also the cattle's medical needs.

As for Colt, he didn't mind the extra work. He actually welcomed the constant distractions that came with overseeing the horse barn. However, hurrying from one task to the next hadn't been enough to push his thoughts away from Sophia this long day.

Everything about their evening together had surprised him. Especially the ending. Whether his eyes were wide open or squeezed shut, he could still remember the softness of her lips against his cheek and the sweet scent of violets in her hair. At that moment, when she'd been so close, he'd wanted to wrap her in his arms and give her a real kiss. One that would have her sighing and longing for more. A kiss that would lead to...

Trouble. Sure, if you work hard at it, you might seduce Sophia into your bed. But what would that accomplish? Other than ultimately hurting her and making you look like a heartless heel?

Sophia wasn't the free-spirited sort who'd settle for an affair with a man, Colt thought, as the mocking voice rambled around in his head. She was the settling down type. Just the kind of woman he wasn't looking for. So he needed to forget about kissing her and focus on the work that was waiting on him.

He was making one last tour through the horse barn when someone called to him from the back of the building.

Turning, he spotted Holt and Blake motioning for him to join them.

Striding back to where the two men were standing, Colt said, "I didn't know you guys were anywhere around. I was about to head home and leave Jim in charge for the night."

"That's fine. But you can't go just yet," Holt said with a big grin. "Not until you see what Mom has bought for the ranch."

"What Holt really means is we're going to be asking you for more of your help around here," Blake added with a sly grin.

"Doing what? Rounding up the remuda on the back section of the ranch?"

Laughing, Holt said, "If the wranglers can't handle that chore without your help, we need to get a new crew."

Chuckling, Colt looked from one man to the other. "So what do you need from me?"

Blake said, "Luke tells us that you're pretty good at handling a team of horses."

"He did? That's generous of him, but I wouldn't say I was good at the job. I've driven a team a few times hitched to a hay wagon. And once I drove a team and buckboard in a rodeo parade."

Holt slapped his shoulder. "You won't have to do anything that nerve-racking."

Blake coughed, and Holt added with a sly chuckle, "Uh, guess that depends on what kind of things get on your nerves."

Before Colt could ask Holt to explain that remark, Blake said, "Let's go outside. It's easier to show you."

The three men walked out the back doors of the

barn. Off to their left, beyond several connecting corrals built of boards, there was an open area for vehicles to travel between the barn and other nearby sheds. Beyond the fencing, Colt could see the shape of something like a wagon.

"What's that? Is Three Rivers going back to hauling hay by team and wagon?" Colt joked.

Clearly amused, Holt said, "This isn't going to be quite that much work."

"We don't think," Blake added with a chuckle.

"Just don't let Mom hear you say that about the hay," Holt warned him. "She might get the idea to try it."

The men made their way past the corrals to where the object was parked behind a flatbed truck. Technically, Colt would have to say he was looking at a wagon. But it was actually a sleigh with wheels underneath.

Colt scratched his chin. "This is a first for me. What do you call this thing?"

"Mom calls it *fun*," Holt said, as though that fully described the object.

"She's been wanting the kids to have sleigh rides for Christmas," Blake explained. "But the few times we've ever had snow it wasn't enough to fill a coffee cup. So this is the next best thing."

"She's purchased the team and harness to go with the sleigh. They're arriving tomorrow," Holt informed him. "Two dapple grays. Sisters, I might add."

Colt walked closer and rested a hand on the short door that opened to a pair of double seats. The upholstery was pristine tuck and roll leather, while the green paint of the main body looked fresh and bright.

Turning a bemused look to the two men, Colt asked, "Are you trying to tell me that I'm going to be the sleigh driver?"

"Ho, ho, ho!" Holt replied, then laughed. "Don't worry, Colt, you don't have to play Santa Claus."

Blake jerked a thumb toward his brother. "I'm thinking Holt should take on the role of Ol' Saint Nick."

"Oh, no!" He patted his flat abs. "I'm in too good physical shape to impersonate Santa."

Blake snorted playfully, then gestured toward the sleigh. "Mom is planning on adding plenty of jingle bells—to go with all the yelling the kids will be doing."

Snickering now, Holt looked at Colt. "Sounds like loads of fun, doesn't it?"

Actually, Colt wasn't thinking about yelling kids or jingle bells. He was too busy imagining Sophia snuggled up to his side and the starlight dusting her pretty face. Yes, taking Sophia for a sleigh ride would be a Christmas gift. It was also a temptation he didn't need in his life.

"I think he's in shock, little brother. He doesn't even hear you."

Blake's voice snapped Colt out of the pleasant reverie, and he grinned happily at the two men.

"Tons of fun!" Colt told them. "I can't wait."

The brothers exchanged dubious looks.

"I'm worried," Holt said. "The man is too agreeable about this."

"Why wouldn't I be?" Colt asked cheerfully. "It's the holiday season. Everyone is supposed to be in a festive mood. I do have a few questions, though. When and where are these rides supposed to take place?"

"You'll have to ask Mom to get those answers," Blake told him. "Why don't you stop by the house on your way home? I'm sure she'll be happy to discuss it with you."

Colt glanced thoughtfully at the ranch house. "I'm sure Maureen is getting ready to eat dinner. I wouldn't want to disturb her."

Blake glanced pointedly at his watch. "She and Gil are probably in the den getting ready for drinks. I promise you, Colt, you won't be disturbing them. But be ready. They will force a cocktail on you," he added.

"Hmm. Well, it's been a long day," Colt said. "A bit of whiskey might loosen up my back. That little dun filly was really mean to me."

Holt laughed and elbowed his brother in the ribs.

"See, I'm not the only one around here that hits the dirt."

"And likes bourbon, too," Blake added with a wry grin. "You horse trainers are all alike."

Colt had heard that in the years before he'd married Isabelle, Holt had been quite the ladies' man. According to some of the hands around the horse barn, their boss had changed women as often as he changed boots. And to hear them tell it, he'd owned dozens of pairs. Even though Holt's rambling ways were all in the past, the gossip had made Colt think about his own dating history back in New Mexico. Luke had often accused him of going through women like a stack of brownies and that one too many would eventually ruin his appetite.

Colt should have listened to his brother's warning. Because he had lost his appetite for female companionship. That is, until he'd looked up and spotted Sophia handing out Christmas cookies to the ranch hands.

He didn't know what the future held, but he did know he was ready to see Sophia again. And stopping by the ranch house to talk with Maureen might just give him the opportunity.

Chapter Five

Sophia drizzled a glaze dressing over the mixture of greens, mandarin oranges and walnuts before giving the contents in the huge wooden bowl a quick toss.

"Mmm. That looks delicious," Jazelle said, peering over Sophia's shoulder. "Did Reeva teach you how to make that?"

Smiling, Sophia said, "Not exactly. But she's the one who first got me interested in cooking. Before I met her, I didn't know anything about preparing food."

"I don't believe I've ever heard you say when you did finally meet your grandmother. Were you already a grown woman by then?"

"No. I was about fifteen when Mom finally allowed me to travel here to Arizona to visit Gran. Before then, the most I knew about cooking was opening a can of soup or putting something frozen in the oven. Mom hated anything to do with the kitchen, so I didn't have anyone to teach me."

Jazelle smirked. "I know the feeling. My mom didn't want me doing anything in the kitchen. Everything had to remain spotless. But back to you, how did you learn so much from Reeva?"

"Each summer I'd spend as much time as I could with Gran. She made cooking seem like an art and I was instantly infatuated with everything about it. To tell you the truth, I probably grated her nerves by asking her so many questions."

"Hmm. I doubt that. And I should've known you got all this love of cooking from Reeva. Like grandmother, like granddaughter."

"Well, my skills are hardly chef caliber. But back in LA I did take a few cooking lessons in between my college classes. So I know enough to back up Gran in the kitchen," she said with a chuckle.

Jazelle pointed to the bowl of salad. "You obviously know plenty. And I think the kids might actually want to eat salad tonight."

"I hope you're right." Sophia handed the bowl to Jazelle in order for the housekeeper to load it on a serving cart. "But if this flops with everyone, I'll take all the blame."

"For what?"

Maureen's voice prompted both Sophia and Jazelle to turn to find the Hollister matriarch standing a few short steps away. Since Maureen often stopped by the kitchen to discuss meal plans or simply have a cup of coffee with Reeva and Sophia, her appearance wasn't a surprise. But the sight of the tall, dark cowboy standing at her side was definitely a shock to Sophia.

What was Colt doing here?

The question raced through Sophia's mind as she tried to form a sensible response to Maureen's question.

Jazelle must have sensed that Sophia had become momentarily tongue-tied, because she quickly answered for her. "Sophia is worried the salad she made might not go over with everyone."

Maureen waved a dismissive hand toward Sophia. "I'm not a bit worried about anything you make, Sophia. You're a chop off the old block."

From her spot in front of the stove, Reeva snapped, "Who's calling who old around here?"

Maureen laughed, and as the two women exchanged a bit more playful banter, Sophia allowed her gaze to settle on Colt. His hat was in his hands, and his jeans and blue denim shirt were brown with dust. Fatigue marked his face and slumped his shoulders. His appearance, coupled with the fact that he was here at the ranch house, made Sophia wonder if there'd been some sort of problem at the horse barn.

His gaze met hers, and he smiled. Not in a flirta-tious way, but a smile that said he was genuinely glad to see her. The notion put tiny wings on her heart, and before she realized what she was doing, she was smiling back at him.

"…and Colt has been very busy today so I want him to eat before he goes home."

Catching the last part of Maureen's sentence, So-phia glanced over to where Jazelle had gotten busy pulling plates from the hutch.

"No problem. I'll set another plate for him," the housekeeper assured Maureen.

"Not in the dining room," Maureen told her, then for reasons Sophia could only guess at, she looked straight at her. "He insists he doesn't want to intrude on the family and eat in the dining room with us. I don't imagine you and Reeva would mind him eat-ing here in the kitchen, would you?"

"Won't mind a bit," Reeva wasted no time in an-swering. "Be nice to have a man's company for din-ner. Won't it, Sophia?"

Feeling as though she'd turned into a wooden mannequin, she smiled and nodded. "Uh, yes. He's surely welcome."

Maureen swept a satisfied smile over the whole bunch, then patted his arm. "We'll talk again, Colt, to make a few more plans. And thank you for being such a good sport about the whole thing."

He said, "No problem. My pleasure, Maureen."

As she departed the kitchen, Reeva walked over and grabbed Colt by the arm.

"You come right over here, Colt, and I'll fill a plate for you. We're having tossed salad, cabbage rolls, pinto beans and corn bread muffins. Does any of that sound to your liking?"

He gave her a wide smile. "Everything sounds great to me, Reeva. But don't stop what you're doing to serve me. I'll wait until you and Sophia can eat with me."

Sophia watched Reeva lead him over to a booth-style table and bench seats, while wondering what had come over her grandmother. She seemed actually happy that Colt had appeared unexpectedly. Normally, she'd be snapping and complaining about being interrupted at the busiest time of the evening.

"That's especially nice of you, Colt," Reeva told him. "You're a real gentleman."

Jazelle paused in her task of gathering dishes to give Sophia a raised eyebrow. With her back to Reeva and Colt, Sophia made a hands-up gesture to indicate to Jazelle that she didn't have a clue as to what had come over her grandmother.

"Sophia, get this man a cup of coffee so he'll have something to do while he waits," Reeva told her.

"Sure, Gran."

By the time Sophia poured the coffee, Colt had settled himself comfortably in the booth, and Reeva had returned to the stove to ladle a portion of the cabbage rolls into a serving dish.

Sophia placed the coffee in front of him, and he responded with a sheepish grin. "Sorry about putting you out like this, Sophia. I didn't mean for this to happen. I stopped by to discuss a matter with Maureen, and she insisted I stay and eat."

"Don't be sorry. You're not putting us out at all. We always prepare more than enough food." She placed a small tray holding a matching stainless-steel sugar bowl and a tiny cream pitcher on the table in front of him. "Make yourself at home, and Gran and I will be finished soon and join you."

"Thanks. This is nice," he told her.

Sophia turned away from the table and drew in a deep, bracing breath. Throughout the day, she'd been telling herself that the time she'd spent with Colt last night had been nothing more than a pleasant outing. She'd been assuring herself that she'd only kissed his cheek out of politeness and nothing more.

But now that he was here in the kitchen and her eyes had made another hungry feast of his rugged image, she knew exactly how much she'd been deluding herself. She'd loved every minute she'd spent with Colt. And she'd desperately wanted to do more than kiss his cheek. She'd wanted to slide her arms around his neck and kiss him like a woman kisses a man when she really wants him.

"Sophia, get the muffins out of the oven before

they burn, and what about the sweet tea? Do you have it brewed and ready to go?"

Sophia grabbed a padded mitten off the cabinet and hurried to the oven. "Yes, Gran. I'll see to all of it."

For the next few minutes she buzzed around the room helping Jazelle load the last of the food onto the serving cart. Once the housekeeper departed the kitchen, she went to gather plates and silverware for Colt, her grandmother and herself.

"Gran, you go ahead and sit down with Colt," she told Reeva. "I'll bring your plate to you."

Reeva switched off all the burners, then headed straight to the coatrack standing next to the back door. "Thank you, honey, but I'm going home."

Dismayed, Sophia stared at her grandmother. "Going home? Why? You haven't eaten yet."

Reeva waved a dismissive hand. "I just thought of something I need to do at home before bedtime. You two go ahead. I've dished up a container to take with me."

From his seat at the table, Colt said jokingly, "Reeva, I know I smell like horse manure, but surely you can stand to be around me long enough to eat."

Buttoning her coat, she glanced over her shoulder at him. "Believe me, Colt, I've smelled a lot worse than you in my day. No. As much as I like your company, the idea of putting my feet up on the couch is even better. Good night, you two."

Before Sophia or Colt could say more, Reeva went out the door. Cold air rushed in as it shut behind her, along with an awkward moment of silence. What was going on with her grandmother? Reeva always ate before she went home for the night.

"Well, something must've come over her awfully fast." Sophia stared thoughtfully at the closed door, then looked over to Colt. "It's not like Gran to leave this early. Do you think she's okay? She didn't look sick to you, did she?"

Colt shook his head. "She looked like a picture of health to me. I think she left because of me."

"Nonsense. I can tell she likes you. A lot."

"I think so, too. That's why she found an excuse to leave," he said. "She thought I wanted to be alone with you."

Sophia's breath momentarily caught in her throat, and then she finally managed to ask, "Did you? I mean, want to be alone with me?"

A grin slowly lifted one corner of his lips. "I like Reeva, but I'm glad she's a savvy woman. I do want to be alone with you."

"Oh." The one word rushed past her lips as a warm blush stung her cheeks.

"Don't tell me that surprises you."

"Well…we only met two days ago."

"A lot can happen in two minutes, even two hours. So two days is an eon—to me."

How could she argue his point? It had taken her

all of two seconds to look into his black eyes and feel a deep-down jolt.

Not daring to make a reply to that, she gestured for him to rise to his feet. "Come on. I've already put our plates by the stove. I'll let you get whatever you'd like."

"I'm right behind you," he told her.

She filled her plate, and while he took care of his own, she poured two iced glasses full of sweet tea. By the time she'd carried everything over to the table, he joined her, and they sat down on opposite sides, facing each other.

"I was picturing myself baking frozen pizza for my dinner tonight," he commented. "I didn't have any idea this was going to happen."

Sophia momentarily forgot about eating as she watched him sow black pepper over the mounds of food on his plate. There were lines of fatigue beneath his dark eyes, and his black hair had fallen in rumpled waves over one eye. And all she could think was how much she'd like to smooth the tips of her fingers over the crescent-shaped indentions beneath his eyes and brush the hanks of hair off his forehead.

Trying not to dwell on that urge, she said, "Maureen isn't going to let anyone leave the house without feeding them. Especially at dinner time."

He dug his fork into his salad bowl. "Actually, I didn't know I was going to be seeing Maureen this evening. But Blake and Holt wanted me to speak with her. She has a…" He paused and chuckled.

"Problem?" Sophia asked before he could continue.

His chuckle turned into a laugh. "No. Somehow she learned through Luke's big mouth that I can drive a team of horses. Now she's planning for me to give all her grandchildren sleigh rides. For Christmas. Jingle bells and dashing through the snow. Only we'll be dashing through the cacti and Joshua trees."

Sophia stared in at him in wonder. "For real? A sleigh?"

He nodded. "Actually, it's a wagon made to look like a sleigh. With the unlikely chance we'll see snow, this sleigh has skids, but they're only for looks. It's actually fitted with wheels beneath the carriage."

"What about reindeer? Dancer and Prancer and Rudolph? Do you really know how to drive a team of reindeer?" She pulled a mischievous face at him as she forked up a mandarin orange. "Or I should say a team of horses pretending to be reindeer?"

He nodded. "Maureen didn't hold back. She purchased two dapple gray mares to go with the sleigh. They're arriving tomorrow. And yes, Luke wasn't exaggerating. Driving a team was something I thought would be fun to do, so several years ago, I learned how from an old cowboy who worked on the T Bar T."

Clapping her hands with glee, she said, "What a wonderful thing to do for the holiday! Leave it to Maureen to come up with something special for the kids." In her excitement, she leaned slightly across the table toward him. "Do you think it would be okay if I pretended to be a kid and take a ride with you?"

His eyes were suddenly glinting. "It would be very okay. You'll be my little elf helper."

"Yay! And I don't even have to go to the North Pole!" she exclaimed with a little laugh. "What about wearing pointy shoes and cap? Is that necessary?"

"That isn't in my rule book. Unless you want to wear pointy shoes," he added with a mischievous wink. "Thank goodness Maureen isn't insisting I wear a Santa suit."

"Oh, I don't know. I think you'd make a great Santa," Sophia said and winked playfully back at him.

"Thanks for the compliment. But I'd appreciate it if you don't give Maureen any more ideas," he said and chuckled. "She seems to come up with plenty on her own."

"Don't worry. I won't suggest that you play Saint Nick. And I won't say anything about the sleigh around any of the children. Because I'm sure Maureen wants this to be a surprise."

He nodded, then changing the subject, glanced around the room. "How's all the extra cooking going?"

"We baked twenty dozen cookies this afternoon." She swallowed a bite of cabbage roll. "I don't think I'll be wanting to eat any cowboy cookies for a long time."

Casting a sly grin at her, he reached for one of the corn bread muffins from a basket Sophia had placed on the table. "Don't tell me you ate a cookie each time a batch came out of the oven."

She groaned. "I didn't eat even one. I have great self-discipline…most of the time," she added impishly. Especially when the temptation was food, she thought. But with a man like Colt, she couldn't be sure. How could she be? She'd never met a man like him before.

"I'll be honest. When I first saw you walk into the kitchen with Maureen, I was afraid you'd been having trouble at the barn," she told him. "I'm glad my initial thoughts were wrong."

"No problems. Just plenty of work. We had two foals born today. A colt and a filly. They're both gorgeous little things." He slanted a thoughtful glance at her. "You ought to come down to the barn and take a look at them."

Before she could reply to his suggestion, he said, "But you might not be into horses that much. You'll have to overlook me, Sophia. From the time I was about this high—" he held a hand above the floor to indicate the height of a very small child "—they've been my life. I get excited over the new babies."

Yes, she could see his excitement, Sophia thought. The moment he'd begun talking about the new foals, his eyes glowed, and the lines of weariness on his face relaxed somewhat.

"Actually, I'd love to see the babies. I, uh, just don't want to be a nuisance or get in the way."

A grin created a dimple in his left cheek, and Sophia figured with his rugged good looks he'd probably had a line of girls chasing after him since his junior-high-school days. And she doubted the line had lessened any over the years. Colt was clearly a man who'd always run just a step faster in order to keep from getting caught. The notion should be enough to keep her attention off the shape of his lips and the dimples in his cheeks, but nothing seemed to dampen this fascination she'd suddenly developed for this man.

He said, "Great! As soon as we're finished with dinner, I'll drive us back to the barn."

It was a good thing she was in the process of biting into a piece of corn bread. Otherwise, her mouth would've fallen open. "Oh, but I have to finish cleaning the kitchen and dealing with leftovers. And the family hasn't even been served dessert yet! I'd feel awful to make you to wait around on me."

He shot her a droll look. "Well, it's only right that you should feel awful. I mean, this is mighty rough on me sitting here in this nice warm kitchen, eating delicious food and talking to a pretty girl. If the pressure was any worse, I don't know that I could stand it."

A blush warmed her cheeks. "Okay. But don't start whining about the time, or I'll remind you that you had warning."

He smiled, and as his black eyes met hers, she felt like a tiny ballerina was behind her breastbone doing a procession of wild pirouettes.

"In case you didn't know, the number one thing a horseman has to have to succeed at his job is patience," he told her. "When you're training a horse, the slow way is really the fastest way. So waiting is my middle name."

"Colt Waiting Crawford," she repeated in a teasing tone. "I kind of like that. It has a nice ring to it."

He laughed and the pleasure she got from the sound of it caused a warning bell to clang in her head. For the past year and a half, she'd fiercely guarded her heart. Now, in a matter of two days, Colt was causing the protective wall she'd erected around her feelings to crack. Much more time with him and the whole thing would probably come crashing down, and her with it.

An hour and a half later, after Colt did what he could to help Sophia deal with the leftovers and tidy up the kitchen, the two of them donned their jackets and walked out into the cool, still night.

At the gate to the backyard fence, Colt glanced up at the star-strung sky and wondered if it was luck or fate that had brought him to this moment with Sophia. When he'd stopped by the house to speak with Maureen, the most he'd been hoping for was a quick hello and maybe to exchange a few brief words with

Sophia. Getting this unexpected time with her had made him forget all about the long, exhausting day.

"It's such a nice evening," he said. "What do you say we walk down to the horse barn? Or are you too tired?"

She shook her head. "I haven't worked that hard. I feel great. And I love to walk."

He'd already noticed she was a good sport about most anything that he suggested. Her agreeable attitude was a pleasant change from the women he'd dated in the past. Most of them would have already objected loudly.

After fastening the gate behind them, he moved to her side and as they began walking in the direction of the ranch yard, he gently wrapped an arm around the back of her waist. "You're a real trooper, Sophia."

"Thanks. Although, I'm not sure I deserve the compliment."

Even through the thin fabric of her jacket, he got a sense of her warmth and softness. Just touching her made his steps feel lighter.

"Sure you do," he said. "You're willing to jump in and do your part. Or join in the fun even when you know you're going to get your hands dirty."

"I must get being a trooper from my grandmother. She's always willing to go the extra mile. Which tells me there was something sly about her rushing home like she did." She glanced sheepishly up at him. "If she honestly did go home to give us alone time, I, uh, hope it didn't embarrass you. Believe me, Colt, I've never given her such ideas."

He gently squeezed the side of her waist. "I never thought you had. And I would hardly be embarrassed over something like that. So quit fretting over it. We had a nice dinner together, didn't we?"

"Yes. For the second night in a row," she answered. "If we're not careful we'll make dining together a habit!"

He couldn't stop a sly chuckle from passing his lips. "There wouldn't be any harm in that. Except that I might gain twenty pounds. A no-no for anyone who rides bucking horses." He glanced down at her. "But you know, it just might be worth it."

"Are you flirting, Colt?"

He laughed. "Well, sort of. Do you always just blurt out what's on your mind?"

She laughed with him. "If I spoke all my thoughts out loud, I'd be in trouble all the time."

He snuggled her closer to his side and felt a spurt of triumphant joy when she didn't pull away.

By now they were passing the long log building that served as the bunkhouse, and she gestured to the smoke rising above the rock chimney at one end of the roof.

"I've noticed the guys have been having fires on most evenings. Where do they get the wood to burn? There's not exactly an abundance of timber around brother? Worried that he might have heatstroke and not make it to your house? Let me tell you, if Santa ⸻ ⸻ ⸺ of your bad behavior. Not ⸻ ⸺ from the heat."

⸻ ⸺ on, Luke. I'm always good. Just ask Dad."

Luke stepped around the paint mare he'd been riding and began to loosen the girth on the saddle. "You have Dad fooled. Along with half of the female population back in New Mexico."

Colt let his brother's comment slide. Even though there was a grain of truth in his comment, Luke was mostly joking. Colt had gone through his share of girlfriends. He could admit that. He could also say he had not purposely tried to fool any of them into thinking his intentions toward them were serious.

"I guess you know that you've really fixed things up for me this Christmas," Colt said as he casually leaned a hip against the rail and lifted his hat just enough to let the breeze cool the top of his head.

"I have? How did I manage to do that?" Luke asked.

He groaned. "You told the Hollisters that I could drive a team of horses."

"So? Is anything wrong with that? Holt mentioned to me that he needed someone who could handle a team. I told him you were the man."

"Yeah, right," Colt said with a good-hearted chuckle. "Now I've been delegated to sleigh driver."

Resting his arms on the seat of the saddle, Luke looked across the horse's back and over to his brother. "You can't fool me. You'd be disappointed if Maureen gave the job to someone else. Knowing you, you've already been picturing yourself as Cowboy Santa. The first and only, naturally."

Colt went to work removing the saddle on the bay gelding he'd been riding. As he unbuckled the breast collar and tossed it over the rail, he said, "You really think I'm that much of a ham?"

"No. But I like to tease my little brother."

Yes, Luke had always teased Colt. He'd also loved, guided and protected his younger brother through the years. The two of them had always been extra close. If Luke hadn't first made the move here to Three Rivers, Colt was certain he'd still be back at the T Bar T.

Which meant he would never have met Sophia. After the kiss they'd shared in the barn last night, she was all he could think about. The passion he'd felt for her had been so hot and sudden that he'd been momentarily blindsided by it. And he'd gotten the impression that she'd been a bit stunned by the whole thing, too. What did it mean for him and for her? That he needed to keep a safe distance between them?

Hell no! She wasn't like the one-night stands he'd enjoyed back in New Mexico. Nor was she comparable to the more responsible women he'd dated on a frequent basis. She was everything sweet and good.

She made him feel like he was riding on a cloud. Why should he give that up?

Because you're not a family man, Colt. You view a woman as your entertainment. You don't want a wife or kids. You never have.

The mocking voice in his head was wrong. Dead wrong! He didn't view Sophia as entertainment. She was worthy of love and respect. But could he step up and be the man to give her everything she deserved and wanted?

"Colt! You need to go to a hearing specialist. I'm fairly certain you've lost yours!"

Luke's voice suddenly interrupted his straying thoughts, and he looked blankly at his brother. "Were you saying something?"

Luke rolled his eyes. "I said you've lost your hearing!"

"No. Before that."

Luke pulled the saddle off the mare's back and placed it atop the rail before he stepped over to Colt. "I was asking what you told Maureen about the sleigh business. Or have you talked to her about it yet?"

"Oh. Sure, I told her I'd be happy to take the kids around the ranch. I'm going to let her choose the routes and the schedule."

Luke's eyes narrowed to skeptical slits as he studied Colt's face. "Are you okay, little brother? I get the impression you're off in la-la land. Did you go to the Fandango last night and drink a bunch of beer?"

Colt frowned at him. "Heck no! Do I look hungover or something?"

"Or something," Luke said drolly.

"Hmm. Must be all those sweets I ate last night. When I stopped at the ranch house last night to speak with Maureen, she insisted I stay for dinner. Sophia served me two helpings of cobbler. Apple and peach."

"Sophia? Jazelle usually serves all the food. Wasn't she there?"

"She was there. But I chose to eat in the kitchen with Sophia. Maureen didn't mind," he added with a coy grin.

"Oh, I see. So you've already set your sights on Sophia," Luke said, then followed the disapproving comment with a shake of his head. "That could get real nasty, Colt."

Annoyed, Colt glared at him. "Nasty? Because I like a girl? Come on, Luke! I know you're an old married man now, but surely your thinking hasn't become that narrow yet."

"You're the one who ought to be thinking, Colt. For the past year you've been harping about women and how you don't care if you go another year without a date. That tells me you're not ready for any kind of meaningful relationship. Her grandmother is like family to the Hollisters. They are bound to be protective of Sophia. If bad feelings ended up between the two of you, it could put you in an awkward position."

This time Colt rolled his eyes. "Listen to you! I

here. And I've noticed the small amounts of firewood for sale in town are extremely expensive."

"It's like burning gold, because wood is such a scarce commodity here in the desert. But the Hollisters own quite a large spread of land near Prescott. I've not seen any of it yet, but the hands tell me they've been clearing mesquite trees on some areas of the place. They haul the cut wood back down here to use in the ranch house and the bunkhouse."

"I didn't realize the Hollisters owned land up there. If you added that to Three Rivers and their other ranch down near Dragoon, it would equal thousands of acres."

"An eye-popping amount," he replied.

"I can't imagine owning that much property. Much less all the valuable livestock."

"Hmm. When Luke first moved here and took the job as Holt's assistant, he tried to describe the ranch to me. My brother has never been the sort to exaggerate, but I thought he had to be spreading it on a bit. No place could be the size of Three Rivers. But I was wrong."

She glanced in his direction. "Do you have a goal to own land some day? Or doesn't that interest you?"

He shrugged one shoulder. "Sometimes I think about getting my own place. Then I ask myself if I'd really be doing the smart business thing. The Hollisters pay me a generous salary. If I was working for myself, it would take years to make a profit equal to what I'm earning now. Anyway, I don't need to be my own boss to be happy. If you asked him, Luke would most likely tell you he feels the same way." He glanced down at her. "Now you're probably thinking I don't have much ambition."

She shook her head. "Not at all. Ambition is good. If you're using it to become a better person, or to help others. It's not good if your ambition is all for self-gain."

A flat tone had crept into her voice as she'd spoken those last few words, and the sound set Colt to wondering who and what she was referring to. Herself, her mother or a man. It had to be one of the three, he decided.

"You say that like you've had a firsthand experience," he said.

She stopped in her tracks and turned to face him. With her head tilted slightly back, her face was sprinkled with stardust, and Colt thought how much he'd like to kiss each glowing spot upon her skin.

"I have, Colt. And it's not something I like talking about. But you brought up the subject of ambition, and since you'll probably hear this anyway, I might as well tell you. About a year and a half ago, I was engaged to be married. My fiancé was an extremely ambitious man, a lawyer working his way up in the firm. And because of all his drive toward the top, Mom thought he was perfect. Mr. Wonderful all around." Her eyes blinked, and her lips flattened into a tight grimace. "He had the wrong kind of want-to in him, Colt. It was for him and him only. I don't believe that's how a person should live, just for themselves."

Colt couldn't imagine her getting tangled up with such a self-centered man. And he hated to think of her being so hurt and disillusioned over a man she'd obviously loved. But most of all, he was very glad she'd broken ties with the creep.

"That's too bad, Sophia. I'm sure you didn't see any of that coming."

"No."

"Sometimes things just don't work out," he said, then gently added, "for different reasons."

"Yeah. Especially when you put your trust in the wrong person." She drew in a deep breath and let it out. "But that was my mistake and one I learned from."

"Well, I'm very glad you were strong enough to stand up for what you needed and wanted. Otherwise, you would've ended up doing all the giving."

"I'm glad, too," she said, then surprised him by suddenly reaching for his hand and wrapping her fingers tightly around his.

"We didn't come out here to talk about wrong choices." A faint smile curved her lips. "Let's go see those new babies of yours."

Her revelation about a broken engagement had left all kinds of questions whirling through his head.

But he kept them to himself. Her past love life was none of his business. And why did he need to know why some creep had broken her heart? All he wanted was to enjoy her company. Not to take notes on her personal history.

Admit it, Colt. There's something in you that wants to know what's going on in her head and her heart.

Shoving away the taunting voice in his head, he said, "I'm all for that."

With his hand secured firmly in hers, the two of them walked on to the barn.

From the moment Sophia had turned to see Colt standing in the kitchen, she'd lost control of her senses and was still struggling to get them back. Why had she told Colt those things about Tristen and her broken engagement? Why was she still holding onto his hand as though he was her lifeline? Or, even worse, her lover? She needed to quit touching him. She needed to stop smiling at him and giving him the idea that she liked him.

Damn it! You do like him, Sophia! You more than like him. Your heart has been doing cartwheels for the past two hours.

The mocking voice was still rattling around in her head as they entered the west end of the barn. But when he led her over to where a sorrel mare and her baby were stalled, she forgot all about letting go of Colt's hand and putting a safe distance between them. Instead, she squeezed his fingers with excitement as she spotted the palomino foal.

"Oh my gosh, how adorable! Look at the curly mane and tail. It's all legs!"

She glanced up to see he was smiling at her with amusement.

"*It* is a boy. A colt. In case you might not know, in the equine world, *colt* means the same as *stallion*," he explained.

She slanted a pointed look at him. "Is that where you got your name?"

He let out a sheepish chuckle, and Sophia couldn't hold back a laugh. "Forgive me, Colt. I couldn't help myself. It was just too easy to tease you."

He playfully pretended to pinch the end of her nose. "My father named me. Or so that's the story he tells. He says that when he took his first look at me, all he could see was a pair of long legs. Like this little guy." He gestured to the palomino baby standing at his mother's side. "And to hear him tell it, my cry didn't sound like a regular baby. It was more like a horse nickering."

Sophia laughed. "You think he might've been stretching the story a bit."

Fond amusement softened his features. "Just a bit."

"Well, true or not, I'd say your father picked the perfect name for you. Colt Waiting Crawford."

Laughing, he looked at her, and the glint she spotted in his dark eyes had her suddenly wondering if the decadent thoughts that were running through her mind were anything close to what he was thinking. Was he imagining how it would feel to put his lips against hers, to experience the sensation of having his strong arms wrapped around her?

The question was making a dizzying circle through her head when his gaze suddenly focused on her mouth.

"Sounds nice when you say it."

"Maybe I should say it again," she murmured, then softly repeated his name.

A tug from his hand turned her toward him, and then his hands slipped to her back. Slowly, he drew her forward until the front of her body was brushing his, and all the while a tiny particle of her brain was screaming at her to pull away and run. But the warning was too puny to have any effect on the rest of her brain. The most she could do was look up and into his dark eyes.

"You seem to remember everything I say, so I'm hoping you won't forget this," he murmured.

She didn't ask him to explain. She was too fascinated by the sight of his head drawing closer to hers, until finally all she could see was the hard line of his lips. And then the meaning of the word *this* became deliciously clear as his lips settled over hers in a slow, intoxicating search.

Colt was kissing her! And oh, all she wanted was

to get closer to him, to feel the heat from his body seep into hers, to feel his lips teasing and plundering her mouth.

Mindlessly, her arms slipped up his chest and curled around his neck. Her lips parted, inviting him to deepen the kiss, and he reacted by pulling her tightly against him, then anchoring her there with strong band of his arms. When his tongue prodded at her teeth, she opened up to allow him the access of her inner mouth.

The intimate connection was enough to set off a hot blaze deep within her body, and the sensation jolted the minute part of her brain that was still working. She didn't just want Colt's kiss, she wanted him to make love to her!

She was wondering where she could possibly find the strength to pull away from him, when he finally lifted his head. The separation of their lips gave her a chance to drag deep breaths of oxygen into her lungs and attempt to gather her senses.

Resisting the urge to lick her swollen lips, she tried to speak. "I, uh, don't think I'll forget that anytime soon."

"Sophia."

Her name was all he said, and then with a hand meshed into her hair, he pulled her head against his chest and held her like that for long moments.

With her cheek pressed to the region of his heart, she could hear it beating fast and hard. The rhythm matched that of her own, and she wondered if their kiss had shaken him as much as it had jolted her.

"You probably think I'm a real jerk."

The rueful note in his voice had her wondering if he was already regretting their impulsive kiss.

She didn't bother to look at him. She didn't want to move and disturb the spell of being in his embrace. "Does kissing me make you a jerk? That's a little insulting, Colt."

"I didn't mean it that way. I meant…well, I don't want you to think I go around trying to seduce a woman I've only known for a few days."

Of course he didn't, she thought wryly. There was no need for him to put out the effort. The moment she'd taken one look at his dark eyes and half grin, she'd been lost. She should feel humiliated for being so weak and willing. But she didn't. For the past year, she'd tried to convince herself that she never again wanted to experience a man's touch or have his kiss lift her to a blissful plane. But she'd been lying to herself.

Easing her head back, she looked questioningly up at him. "Is that what you're trying to do? Seduce me?"

A faint smile tilted the corners of his lips, and as she studied their hard, masculine curves, she wanted to taste them all over again.

"No. I'm trying to hang on to my sanity," he told

her. "Because if I hadn't kissed you I was going to lose my wits."

"That has to be one of the corniest lines I've ever heard."

His smile widened. "Go ahead and laugh. I won't mind."

Her breath caught in her throat as he pulled one arm from behind her back and used his forefinger to trace a circle upon her cheek.

"I don't want to laugh," she told him. "I want us to go see the other foal, before you decide you need to save your sanity—again."

And put hers in dire jeopardy, she thought.

Chuckling under his breath, he bent his head and placed a soft kiss on the middle of her forehead.

"You're the sweetest, Sophia."

She was trying to decide how she could possibly respond to that remark, when he curved an arm around the back of her shoulders and turned her in the opposite direction of where they were standing.

"Come on, the other baby is over here on the opposite side of the barn."

As he guided her away from the stall and across the wide alleyway, Sophia wasn't sure if she was feeling disappointed or relieved. Yet at this point it hardly mattered, she thought. His kiss had already turned her world upside down.

Chapter Six

Most every day on Three Rivers was sunny, but the next morning it seemed to be shining even brighter. By the time Luke and Colt had put several horses through a series of training exercises in the outside arena, the temperature had inched upward to make it feel more like spring than December.

Now, as the brothers stood at a hitching rail at the back of the arena, Colt used his sleeve to wipe droplets of sweat from his forehead.

"If the weather is this warm at Christmas, Santa will have to change his fur suit to something cooler," he said.

Luke grunted with amusement. "What's wrong,

brother? Worried that he might have heatstroke and not make it to your house? Let me tell you, if Santa ░░░░░░░░░░░░░░ ░ ░ of your bad behavior. Not ░░░░░░░ ░░░ ░ from the heat."

░░ ░░░ ░░░ on, Luke. I'm always good. Just ask Dad."

Luke stepped around the paint mare he'd been riding and began to loosen the girth on the saddle. "You have Dad fooled. Along with half of the female population back in New Mexico."

Colt let his brother's comment slide. Even though there was a grain of truth in his comment, Luke was mostly joking. Colt had gone through his share of girlfriends. He could admit that. He could also say he had not purposely tried to fool any of them into thinking his intentions toward them were serious.

"I guess you know that you've really fixed things up for me this Christmas," Colt said as he casually leaned a hip against the rail and lifted his hat just enough to let the breeze cool the top of his head.

"I have? How did I manage to do that?" Luke asked.

He groaned. "You told the Hollisters that I could drive a team of horses."

"So? Is anything wrong with that? Holt mentioned to me that he needed someone who could handle a team. I told him you were the man."

"Yeah, right," Colt said with a good-hearted chuckle. "Now I've been delegated to sleigh driver."

Resting his arms on the seat of the saddle, Luke looked across the horse's back and over to his brother. "You can't fool me. You'd be disappointed if Maureen gave the job to someone else. Knowing you, you've already been picturing yourself as Cowboy Santa. The first and only, naturally."

Colt went to work removing the saddle on the bay gelding he'd been riding. As he unbuckled the breast collar and tossed it over the rail, he said, "You really think I'm that much of a ham?"

"No. But I like to tease my little brother."

Yes, Luke had always teased Colt. He'd also loved, guided and protected his younger brother through the years. The two of them had always been extra close. If Luke hadn't first made the move here to Three Rivers, Colt was certain he'd still be back at the T Bar T.

Which meant he would never have met Sophia. After the kiss they'd shared in the barn last night, she was all he could think about. The passion he'd felt for her had been so hot and sudden that he'd been momentarily blindsided by it. And he'd gotten the impression that she'd been a bit stunned by the whole thing, too. What did it mean for him and for her? That he needed to keep a safe distance between them?

Hell no! She wasn't like the one-night stands he'd enjoyed back in New Mexico. Nor was she comparable to the more responsible women he'd dated on a frequent basis. She was everything sweet and good.

She made him feel like he was riding on a cloud. Why should he give that up?

Because you're not a family man, Colt. You view a woman as your entertainment. You don't want a wife or kids. You never have.

The mocking voice in his head was wrong. Dead wrong! He didn't view Sophia as entertainment. She was worthy of love and respect. But could he step up and be the man to give her everything she deserved and wanted?

"Colt! You need to go to a hearing specialist. I'm fairly certain you've lost yours!"

Luke's voice suddenly interrupted his straying thoughts, and he looked blankly at his brother. "Were you saying something?"

Luke rolled his eyes. "I said you've lost your hearing!"

"No. Before that."

Luke pulled the saddle off the mare's back and placed it atop the rail before he stepped over to Colt. "I was asking what you told Maureen about the sleigh business. Or have you talked to her about it yet?"

"Oh. Sure, I told her I'd be happy to take the kids around the ranch. I'm going to let her choose the routes and the schedule."

Luke's eyes narrowed to skeptical slits as he studied Colt's face. "Are you okay, little brother? I get the impression you're off in la-la land. Did you go to the Fandango last night and drink a bunch of beer?"

Colt frowned at him. "Heck no! Do I look hungover or something?"

"Or something," Luke said drolly.

"Hmm. Must be all those sweets I ate last night. When I stopped at the ranch house last night to speak with Maureen, she insisted I stay for dinner. Sophia served me two helpings of cobbler. Apple and peach."

"Sophia? Jazelle usually serves all the food. Wasn't she there?"

"She was there. But I chose to eat in the kitchen with Sophia. Maureen didn't mind," he added with a coy grin.

"Oh, I see. So you've already set your sights on Sophia," Luke said, then followed the disapproving comment with a shake of his head. "That could get real nasty, Colt."

Annoyed, Colt glared at him. "Nasty? Because I like a girl? Come on, Luke! I know you're an old married man now, but surely your thinking hasn't become that narrow yet."

"You're the one who ought to be thinking, Colt. For the past year you've been harping about women and how you don't care if you go another year without a date. That tells me you're not ready for any kind of meaningful relationship. Her grandmother is like family to the Hollisters. They are bound to be protective of Sophia. If bad feelings ended up between the two of you, it could put you in an awkward position."

This time Colt rolled his eyes. "Listen to you! I

ate a meal with a woman, and you leapfrog ahead to the two of us having a big fight—as if we were a real couple or something."

Luke's forehead wrinkled with a frown before he abruptly turned and untied the mare's halter rope from the rail. "Okay. I'm getting way ahead of myself. Sorry. I should never have mentioned anything about it. But I lived through it with Pru. She and Blake's wife, Kat, are like sisters. Before we were married, we went through a sour stretch, and it made things uncomfortable for all of us."

Colt understood exactly what Luke was trying to say, but he didn't need his advice. He wasn't planning on getting *that* serious with Sophia.

"I don't mean to sound prickly, Luke. I know your advice is well meaning. Can't I just enjoy a woman's company without you getting all worried about it?"

"You've broken a few hearts, Colt."

"Not on purpose. I can't help it if those women had more feelings for me than I did for them. Heck, I never promised them anything."

"Except a good time," Luke said flatly.

What could Colt say to that? Except that he didn't need his brother to tell him that Sophia wasn't the sort to have a meaningless affair.

"Finished with the mare, Luke? I'll put her up."

Colt looked around to see Jim walking toward them. The middle-aged ranch hand was as dependable as the sun rising in the morning and never failed to be around whenever he was needed. From what Luke had told him, Jim had once been married, but his wife had died in some sort of accident. Colt was surprised that Luke knew that much about the man. What little talking Jim did with anyone was always about work.

Luke handed the mare's lead rope over to the cowboy. "Thanks, Jim. Just put her in the paddock with the older mares."

"Right. It'll take her about five minutes in there to learn all about pecking order," Jim said with a chuckle.

He walked away with the mare in tow, and Luke turned back to Colt. "It's nearly lunchtime. I think I'll go on to the barn and eat. Want to join me?"

Colt said, "No. I'm not that hungry yet. I think I'll get the dun filly and see if she's still in the mood to buck. I don't want her getting the idea that she's won the challenge."

Luke studied him for a long moment, then let out a heavy sigh. "You're mad at me now. For warning you about Sophia."

Colt shook his head. "I'm not mad or anything close to it. I just want you to understand that I can see Sophia is different from the other women I've dated. And I wouldn't hurt her for anything. She's already been hurt enough."

Luke arched a questioning brow at him. "I suppose she told you this?"

"She did. And I damned sure don't want to cause her more misery than what she's already been through."

A strange expression appeared on Luke's face, and then it suddenly disappeared as he reached out and gave Colt an affectionate slap on the shoulder.

"Sorry, Colt. Guess I'm sounding worse than Dad, when he gets on his high horse and starts lecturing us on what we should and shouldn't do."

"True. Way worse than Dad. But I forgive you," he added with a grin.

Seemingly satisfied that all was well between them, Luke started off toward the barn, then paused and called back to him. "Think you can handle Daisy Mae without me around?"

"I can handle her and any other horse you throw at me," Colt bragged, then added with a laugh, "even if I get a few broken bones in the process."

Luke waved a dismissive hand at him. Then heading on toward the barn, he called over his shoulder, "It's obvious you don't need any help in the self-confidence department."

Wrong, Colt thought, as he watched his brother walk across the disked dirt of the arena. Since he'd met Sophia, he'd begun to experience all sorts of doubts about himself.

Sure, he could entertain and flirt with a woman long enough to keep her happy for a while. But he couldn't see himself keeping a woman content for the long haul. He and Luke had watched their father struggle and sacrifice to keep their mother happy and his family together. In spite of her medical condition, there had been long interludes when she'd been a gentle and loving wife and equally affectionate mother. And Colt supposed those good times made the episodes of when she'd go off her meds even harder for them all to endure. Yet somehow through it all, his father's love for his wife had never wavered, nor his patience to deal with her highs and lows. Colt didn't know if somewhere inside him, he could find such inner strength, or the capacity to love that much.

But when Sophia had stood in his arms and snuggled her head against him as if he was the pillar of strength she'd been needing and wanting in her life, he'd been consumed with a feeling that had been totally foreign to him. That one moment of having her in his arms had started a revolution in his head. Now he wanted to think he could conquer the world for her.

It was stupid. Downright stupid.

"Colt, you want me to put up the bay?"

He looked over his shoulder to see Jim had returned from putting the mare out to pasture.

"Yes," Colt told him. "I'll keep the saddle, and you can put the bay on the walker."

"I'll take him. You stopping for lunch now?"

Colt shook his head. "No. I'm going to ride Daisy Mae."

The cowboy shot him a look that said he needed

his head examined. "Man, you must be feeling reckless today. Or should I say *courageous*," he added with a chuckle.

Funny, but it had taken a lot more courage for him to kiss Sophia than it did to climb on a filly that rolled the whites of her eyes and snorted fire. He knew what was in Daisy Mae's mind and exactly how she planned to treat him. He didn't know what Sophia was really thinking.

"She's going to be special, Jim. But first somebody has to teach her a few manners and it's my job to do that."

Jim lifted his hat and raked a thoughtful hand through his hair. "Isn't that Holt and Luke's job, too?"

Colt pulled the saddle from the bay's back and tossed it over the hitching rail. "Yeah. But me and that dun filly have already become acquainted. I don't want her to start missing me."

Jim reached for the bay's bridle reins. "I'll be back by the time you get her saddled. There's no way in hell I'm going to leave you out here alone with her."

"That isn't necessary, Jim."

"Maybe not. But I'll be back just the same."

"Honey, there's no need for you to fret over your mother. She can't yet accept that you're not at her beck and call. That you're not working as an interior designer anymore. But once she sees you're staying in Arizona for good, she'll give in and quit badgering you. Why don't you turn off the ringer on the phone? You don't need to hear that thing."

Realizing her grandmother was right, Sophia pushed the Mute button before she returned it to the end of the countertop.

"I know exactly what she's doing, Gran. She's trying to make me feel guilty for living my life the way I choose rather than the way she chooses. She's always liked to use guilt as a tool of persuasion. But it's not going to work on me. Not this time."

"Good for you, sweetie. You spoke to her yesterday and assured her you were healthy and happy. She doesn't need to call you ten times today," Reeva said as she coated a rump roast with a mixture of seasonings. "Or, for that matter, any day."

Biting back a sigh, Sophia returned to the work island where she'd been busy for the past hour packing the holiday tins with homemade cookies and candy. She was down to the last five when Maureen entered the kitchen through the back door.

Tall and slender with shoulder-length chestnut hair threaded with silver, Maureen was a vibrant, attractive woman. Even the way she looked now in dusty jeans and boots and a cowboy shirt with the sleeves rolled against her forearms. Unless she had some sort of meeting that sent her to town or kept her tied to the ranch house, she and Gil worked every day on the range with the ranch hands.

Sophia had only been a teenager when she'd seen

Maureen for the first time. The woman had been herding cattle in a holding pen, and dust had been flying everywhere. The horned cattle had been rowdy and aggressive, and Sophia had been terrified that Maureen was going to be horned in the leg or worse. But the woman had handled the task as though it had been a walk in the park. Now Sophia could only imagine how it would feel to have a mother like Maureen. A strong, loving woman who truly wanted her children to be independent rather than puppets to her will.

"Hi, ladies," she greeted as she took off her brown cowboy hat and swatted it against her leg. "Do you have any coffee made? I told the guys I'd bring some thermoses to the cattle barn. We're getting ready to vaccinate a couple hundred head."

"I drained the last of the morning coffee," Reeva said as she carried the roast to the stove and placed it in a large, granite roaster.

"I'll get it going." Sophia hurried across the room to where an industrial-sized coffee maker sat on its own special cabinet. As she began to pull out the makings, she asked, "How many thermoses do you want?"

"Six should be enough," Maureen told her. She moved over to the work island where Sophia had been filling the holiday tins. "Do you have any extra cookies? Or is it going to take all you have for the nursing home gifts?"

"I imagine Sophia can spare a few. She's nearly finished," Reeva said, then glanced over her shoulder at Maureen. "You're spoiling those men."

"Not spoiling. Treating," Maureen corrected her. "It's the holiday season. Besides, happy cowboys always work harder."

She walked over to where Sophia was pulling tall metal thermos bottles from a cabinet below the coffee maker.

"I don't know how I manage to get so many irons in the fire," she said as she massaged the lines of fatigue in her forehead. "I promised the nursing homes I would deliver the cookie tins today, because they're having parties for their residents tomorrow. But after we finish vaccinating the cattle, Gil and I have to hurry up to Prescott to meet with a man from the land management bureau. I guess the cookies will have to wait."

Sophia glanced thoughtfully at Maureen. "This is my afternoon off and I was going into town to do some shopping, anyway. I'd be happy to deliver the tins for you."

Maureen shot her a grateful look. "Oh, that would be great, Sophia. You'll only have to stop at two different retirement homes. It shouldn't take you long."

Reeva spoke up. "If she left right now it would still be dark before she got back here to the ranch. And I don't like the idea of Sophia driving over the ranch road after dark. It's rough and lonely."

"I'll be fine, Gran," Sophia told her grandmother. "Are you sure you can handle cooking dinner without me this evening?"

Reeva snorted. "I've done it for all these years. I think I can manage without you this one time."

Maureen thoughtfully tapped a finger against her chin. "On second thought, I think your grandmother is right, Sophia. You shouldn't make the trip alone."

Reeva placed the roast in the oven and walked over to join them. "Now you're talking, Maureen. She needs someone to go with her. Someone like Colt," she added with a clever grin.

Sophia's jaw dropped as she stared at her grandmother. Why was she playing this matchmaking game? It wasn't her nature, at all! "Oh no, Gran! You—"

Maureen interrupted with a gleeful clap. "Reeva, that's the best thinking you've done in ages. I'm certain Colt would love to accompany Sophia to town."

Sophia gasped. "He's busy at the horse barn. I wouldn't dare ask him! I'll be perfectly fine going alone."

Ignoring that last part, Maureen said, "Okay. If it bothers you that much to ask Colt, I'll do it for you."

Sophia inwardly groaned. This whole issue was getting worse by the minute. "No. I wouldn't want you to do that, Maureen." She let out a sigh of resignation. "I'll ask him. But if he's busy, I'll go it alone."

Maureen smiled smugly. "Don't worry. Colt won't be too busy. I'll tell Holt to make sure of that."

Sophia wanted to groan with frustration, but she tamped back the urge.

"I really don't know what you two are up to," Sophia said as she glanced back and forth between Reeva and Maureen, "but you might as well know right now that trying to throw me and Colt together isn't going to work."

Reeva and Maureen exchanged conspiring glances.

"Why, Sophia, why would we do something like that? You're a smart, talented and beautiful young lady," Maureen told her. "You don't need our help to get a boyfriend. We're just trying to make sure your trip to town and back is a safe one."

A trip with Colt? Safe? Sophia very nearly laughed out loud. She couldn't imagine anything more dangerous than being cooped up in the dark cab of a truck with Colt. And the fear wasn't of him. After their kiss last night she couldn't trust herself to resist him.

Why would you want to, Sophia? The cowboy is a hunk. He makes stars fly behind your closed eyes. Bells ring in your head. Why not enjoy the man while you can?

Because she was afraid, Sophia answered the daring voice whispering through her head. She'd given in to passion with Tristen, and look what that had gotten her. She'd been crushed by his indifference, humiliated by the fact that she'd mistaken sex for love. She couldn't go through that sort of pain a second time.

Sophia smiled wanly. "I'm not looking for a boyfriend," she assured Maureen, then turned a look of disbelief on Reeva. "And Gran, you know that, too! What are you thinking?"

Reeva scowled at her. "I'm thinking you need some fun in your life. Twenty-six years old is too young to stop seeing yourself as a woman!"

If anyone else had made such a comment to her, she would've been horribly embarrassed. As it was, she understood Reeva was saying these things out of love, and so was Maureen. Which only made it more difficult for Sophia to put up a protest.

"Okay, you two, to make you both happy, I'll giggle and bat my eyelashes at Colt."

Laughing, Maureen patted Sophia's cheek. "You're a good sport, Sophia."

"Is that anything like being a real trooper?" she asked.

Maureen looked at her with amused curiosity. "Why, yes, I suppose it is. Why?"

Shaking her head, Sophia turned back to the coffee machine to check whether the brewing was completed.

"Oh, no reason," she told her. "Uh, someone else said that to me, that's all."

Someone who, with only one kiss, had changed

the way she'd been viewing herself and the future, Sophia thought.

If she had any sense, she'd keep her fingers crossed that he would be too busy this evening to bother about accompanying her into Wickenburg.

But where Colt was concerned, she had no sense. None at all.

Since Colt had taken the job at Three Rivers, he'd been working overtime most every day of the week, and the idea of asking for time off had never entered his head. Not because the Hollisters demanded or expected him to keep his nose to the grindstone. Or, in his case, his presence in the horse barn twenty hours a day. But Colt had the same work ethic as his father and brother. It wasn't his nature to leave a job where he might be needed.

When Sophia had called him earlier this afternoon and asked if he could accompany her into town, he'd wanted to let out a happy whoop. On the other hand, he'd hated like hell to ask Holt for someone to fill in for him. Especially when it was Colt's responsibility to see that the barn was safely and securely settled for the night.

But oddly enough, he'd been spared the awkward task. By midafternoon Holt had come to him and insisted he take off work early. Otherwise, Maureen was going to be angry at both of them. Colt had been relieved that the matter had been taken out of his hands, but he'd also been left wondering. Just whose idea had it been for him to go with Sophia tonight? Hers or Maureen's?

Now, hours later, Colt told himself it didn't matter who'd come up with the idea. Either way, he'd been given the chance to be with Sophia, and he intended to enjoy every minute of the time with her.

"I honestly feel awful about this, Colt. I'm sure you had other, more important things to do," she said.

Colt was forced to keep his gaze on the road as he maneuvered the truck around a rocky patch in the road.

"You've already said this, Sophia, back at the ranch house. It was totally unnecessary then, so you hardly need to repeat it. You didn't force me into this."

A few minutes ago, when he'd picked Sophia up at the ranch house and helped her load the boxes of goodies to take to the nursing homes, he'd not expected her to look so lovely. He'd imagined she'd be dressed casually in jeans and a flannel shirt or sweater. Instead, she was wearing a copper-brown skirt that hugged her hips and thighs and stopped halfway down her knee-high boots. A silky cream blouse, buttoned up the front, was tucked into her skirt to highlight the tiny silhouette of her waist.

Her sexy image was making it very hard for Colt to hold his focus on driving. Especially when his eyes wanted to continually shift in her direction.

Shaking her head, she muttered, "Ha! Between my grandmother and Maureen and Holt, you didn't have much option."

He smiled to himself. "Look at me, Sophia. I'm a thirty-year-old man. I've been told that one of the first words I learned to speak was *no*. I haven't forgotten how to say it...if I want to."

"I believe you," she said with a sigh. "But it's still embarrassing."

"Why? To be out with me? Again?"

From the corner of his eye, he saw she was staring at him with her eyes wide and her mouth forming a perfect O.

"No! I enjoy your company, Colt. I just don't like either one of us to be manipulated."

He chuckled. "Think about it, Sophia. All of us go through life being manipulated in one way or another. If we're lucky, we'll get some enjoyment out of it. Like we're going to tonight."

"Are we?"

He couldn't stop himself from chuckling again. "Well, aren't you having fun yet?"

She laughed at that, and Colt was relieved to see her tense shoulders relax against the back of the seat.

"Loads of it," she told him. "So tell me, did you have a busy day with the horses? Were any foals born?"

Just the mention of their time together in the barn last night was all it took to have him reliving the taste of her sweet lips, the special feeling that had poured through him as he'd held her in his arms.

"No new foals today. Why? Were you thinking you'd like to make another trip to the barn?"

"I…" She looked at him. "Are you really asking me if I'd like to see the foals again? Or repeat that kiss?"

His boot almost slipped off the accelerator. Not for one second had he expected her to bring that scorching embrace into the conversation.

"Maybe both," he admitted.

She released a long breath, and though he wished her sigh had been one of longing, it was more like a sound of weary confusion.

That's what you get for trying to woo a woman who's had her heart broken, Colt. She's not ready for romance. And she's certainly not ready to put her faith in the likes of you.

He was trying to push the sarcastic voice from his head when she surprised him with a reply.

"I'll, uh, have to think about that, Colt."

Kissing her again was the only thing Colt had been thinking about. But he wasn't going to confess that to her. Only a fool would let a woman know she already had a hold on him. And he wasn't quite ready to put himself into the chump category.

By the time Colt and Sophia had delivered the boxes of tins to the two nursing homes, it was well after dark, and most of the shops and eating places in town were bustling with people who'd just gotten off work.

As Sophia peered out the passenger window at a part of the business area she'd not had a chance to visit before, she asked, "Did you want to do any shopping before we eat dinner?"

He said, "I have a few people left on my to-buy-for list, but I didn't really plan to do any Christmas shopping tonight. What about you?"

"I need to pick up a few personal items for myself. As for gift-buying, I still haven't made my list." She glanced at her watch. "If you're hungry, I could certainly eat now."

He flashed her a grin, and Sophia felt a flutter in her stomach that had nothing to do with the need for food. So far she'd managed to keep her hands off the man. Too bad she couldn't control her mind. All she could think about was how sexy he looked with his long legs encased in faded jeans, and a denim jacket covering a black western shirt that made his hair and eyes seem that much darker.

He was definitely a walking, talking hunk of cowboy. Yet his rugged features and whipcord body were only a part of the things about him that held her attraction. She had to admit she was drawn to the man inside, and that made being with him even more dangerous to her heart.

"I'm always hungry," he said. "I was actually

tempted to open up one of those tins we delivered and sneak a handful of cookies. But bad boys don't get visits from Santa, so I behaved myself."

She laughed. "I think you fibbed about your age. You're not thirty. You're about eight years old," she teased.

"Sorry. I'll try to put on my serious face and act my real age this evening. I think I have a cane hidden behind the back seat. Will that help to mature my image?"

Grinning now, she shook her head. "You're an idiot. And do you honestly have a cane stored behind the seat?"

"Sure. When you have a job like mine, you never know when you're going to end up injured and need one." His features suddenly took a sober turn. "Like Dad. He'd give me all kinds of hell if he heard me describe him as disabled. He doesn't think of himself that way. And neither do I—not really. Only there are times I wish that things hadn't happened to change his life."

Sophia had never heard such a serious tone in his voice before, and it took her by surprise. "I didn't realize your father was disabled. I recall you saying he still trained horses."

"He does train horses for a ranch in Texas. But he has a prosthetic leg from just below the knee. He, uh, lost it in the accident that killed my mom."

"Oh, Colt. How awful!"

He shrugged. "Things happen. We don't plan on them. And we sure as heck don't want them, but that's just a part of life. Dad has moved far beyond the accident. And I guess you could say that Luke and I have moved on from it, too. But sometimes it still haunts me." He darted a rueful glance at her. "You see, Mom caused the wreck."

Sophia gasped. "Accidently or purposely?"

"Dad isn't sure. As I mentioned, she was bipolar, and as they were driving home she flew into a rage over something trivial. She grabbed the steering wheel, and they got into a tussle. The crash took her life and the bottom half of his leg."

"Oh, I'm so sorry, Colt. Were you very young when it happened?"

"Luke was fifteen and I was thirteen. I guess you could say we were pretty much traumatized for a while, but Dad was, and still is, an iron man. He got us through. Even so, that doesn't keep me from wishing that things could've been different."

"We all have wishes that don't come true. That's a part of life, too."

His gaze remained on the traffic ahead of them. "Unfortunately, you're right."

Things happen that we don't plan on. As Sophia thought about Colt's earlier remark and the tragedy he'd endured with his parents, her hand unconsciously splayed against her lower abdomen. If misfortune hadn't stepped into her life, she would be a mother now, she thought sadly. But having a child hadn't been in the cards for her. Now she wondered if she'd ever have the courage to find a man who'd want to marry her. And, more importantly, one who'd want them to have children.

Doing her best to shake away her doubtful thoughts, she noticed he'd already driven through the busier part of town and had practically reached the outskirts.

"Where are we going?" she asked. "I thought we were going to eat."

"We are. I have a nice Mexican restaurant in mind that I thought you might enjoy. It's a short distance from town."

"Oh. That's okay with me," she said. "But I was going to make a suggestion."

"Suggest away," he told her. "I'm game for anything. Except sushi. I'm not too wild about it. I need my food cooked."

His admission put a smile on her face. "Don't worry. I don't want raw fish. I was thinking I'd love to go to the Broken Spur. That is, if you don't mind eating there."

Without a word, Colt slowed the truck, then after making sure no traffic was behind him, pulled to the side of the highway.

Turning sideways in the seat, he looked at her as if he was sure he'd heard wrong. "Did you say *the Broken Spur*?"

"I did. Why are you looking at me like that?" she asked.

He let out a short laugh. "Honey, you obviously don't know about the Broken Spur. It's—"

"Yes, I do know," she quickly interrupted. "It's a ratty little café that's as old as the hills. It's a place where the local cowboys eat and hang out. And you should know why they gather there. It's because the food is scrumptious."

"Who told you that?"

"Gran. And she's an expert on food. She says every time Camille comes home for a visit she goes to the Broken Spur. And Camille owns her own diner. Those two recommendations are plenty enough to convince me."

"Oh, I don't need recommendations," he assured her. "I've eaten there. They serve basic comfort food, and it is delicious. But when you describe the Broken Spur, you need to emphasize *ratty*. And you're all dressed up."

"So? They'll still let me in like this, won't they?" She gestured to her blouse and skirt.

His answer was a robust laugh, and then suddenly he was reaching across the console and wrapping his hand around hers. The contact was warm and familiar. So was the glint in his eyes. And as Sophia dared to meet his gaze, her breathing slowed until it was practically nonexistent.

"You are so…"

"Silly?" she finished for him.

"No. I was going to say *precious*, Sophia. I've never met any woman like you."

How many women had he told that to? She'd be naive to think she was the first. And yet something in his voice made her believe he was being truthful.

Taking a deep breath, she said, "Well, in case you might be wondering, I've never met anyone like you, either."

A lopsided grin twisted his lips. "I don't imagine you were acquainted with very many cowboys in Los Angeles."

"I didn't mean because you were a cowboy," she admitted. "I meant just you...as a man. You know what I like most about you?"

His fingers tightened ever so slightly on her hand. "I'm afraid to guess."

She said, "You make me laugh. And it's been a long, long time since I've wanted to smile, much less laugh. Thank you for that, Colt."

The glint in his eyes softened to a glow, and for a split second, Sophia considered leaning across the console and placing her lips on his. To be connected to him in that way was like a deep hunger that couldn't be assuaged with food or drink.

"It's my pleasure, Sophia."

She cleared her throat and smiled.

"Does this mean we're going to the Broken Spur?"

"I wouldn't consider going anywhere else."

He released her hand, and as he steered the truck back onto the highway, Sophia was shocked to feel tears stinging the backs of her eyes.

Why was she getting emotional just because Colt had agreed to take her to a ratty café?

Because Tristen would never have done that much for her. He wouldn't have been caught dead going into a nursing home with her and helping her stack the gifts of cookies and candy beneath a Christmas tree. And try as she might, she could never remember him calling her *precious*.

She'd made a horrible mistake for believing Tristen had ever loved her. And God help her, she was going to try with all her might not to make the same crushing mistake with Colt.

Chapter Seven

In spite of it being a work night and past the dinner hour for most people, the graveled parking lot surrounding the Broken Spur was jammed with vehicles.

"Looks like a popular place. I didn't expect it to be this busy," Sophia remarked as the two of them made their way to the front of the dingy stucco building. "Maybe we should've called first for reservations."

He grunted with amusement. "I hope you're kidding."

"I am."

The building was unadorned, with only two small windows bracketing a wooden door. There was no portico to shelter the entrance or even a step at the entrance. In one of the windows, a neon sign glowed a single word: Café. Sophia could only think the proprietor didn't waste any money on aesthetics.

As soon as they stepped inside, Sophia was met with a waft of very warm air carrying the odors of fry grease, coffee and corn tortillas. On the left side of the room, a long bar made of polished wood was lined with cowboys of varying ages. Most of them were wearing hats and spurs, and from the looks of their dusty clothes, they'd come straight off the range. Somewhere behind the bar a radio was playing country Christmas tunes. Along with the clink of silverware against crockery, conversation and laughter punctuated the twangy music.

With a hand against her back, Colt guided her to the only vacant table to be found. The square wooden top was scarred from years of use and abuse. In several places, initials had been carved into the thick pine planks, and when he pulled out one of the chairs for her, the vinyl padded seat was torn down the middle to reveal a layer of white padding. He promptly shoved it back under the table.

"Wait, Sophia, you might snag your skirt. Let's try this one." He pulled out an adjacent chair, only to find the seat in a similar condition.

With a good-natured chuckle, she said, "My skirt will survive. This one will be fine."

"Are you sure you don't want to go somewhere

else for dinner?" he asked as he helped her into the chair.

Smiling up at him, she said, "Not on your life, Colt! I'm getting to experience real cowboy culture."

He sank into the chair angled to her left and after he'd removed his black Stetson and placed it in the vacant seat next to him, he shot her a bemused look. "I'm not even going to try to figure you out. As long as you're happy, I'm happy."

She made a hands-up gesture. "What's there to figure out? Gran taught me to appreciate good food. No matter where or how it's served. And I've heard so much about this place, I thought tonight would be a good time to try it."

An older waitress with hair that graduated from graying roots to a fire engine–red ponytail hurried up to their table. The dry, Arizona climate had created a road map of wrinkles on her face, but the smile she gave Sophia and Colt was genuine. She liked her at once.

"You two out on the town tonight?" she asked.

Colt said, "We've come to enjoy your good food."

The waitress turned a meaningful look on Sophia, then shook her head with disbelief. "Is this the best he could do?" she asked, jerking a thumb in Colt's direction.

Sophia slanted a mischievous grin at Colt. "I pleaded with him, but he gave me a choice. Eat here, or don't eat at all."

The waitress rolled her eyes, then said in a be-moaning voice, "Oh, what we women do for love."

The woman was teasing, of course, but it was clear that she considered Colt and Sophia a couple who were romantically involved. Did the idea embarrass him?

From the corner of her eye, she could see he wasn't blushing or frowning. But he could be silently groaning, she thought.

After the waitress departed to get their drink orders, Sophia reached over and placed her hand over his. "Poor thing. First Gran and Maureen, now the waitress. I'm sorry, Colt. I was only joking with the woman, and she ran with it. I imagine you've reached the end of your patience with me. Even with your middle name being Waiting."

He frowned. "Do you really think I'm that much of a stuffed shirt? I don't know what sort of men you knew in California, but I'm a little more laid-back than that."

"You don't have to tell me that. I can see the sort of guy you are. But a man can only take so much ribbing before he finally blows his stack."

He laughed again, and Sophia was drawn to the joy on his face. During the months she'd been engaged to Tristen, he'd rarely laughed. To be fair, he'd been the serious-minded sort with an equally serious job. Laughing hadn't figured into his life. And in the end, neither had she figured into it. Not completely.

Now as she looked back on their time together, she wondered what had drawn her to him.

"Good thing I took off my hat," he joked. "Otherwise, my blown stack would send it sailing over to the bar and probably knock someone in the head."

She smiled softly at him. "Thanks again, Colt, for reminding me how to laugh."

His gaze caught and held hers. "Had you actually forgotten?"

The tender look in his eyes made their surroundings fade into nothing more than a mixture of muted sound and colors. His rugged face and the low timbre of his voice were the only things registering with her senses.

"I think…for a while I forgot how to do a lot of things," she told him. "But I'm learning how to do them again, and it feels good. Very good."

A shadow suddenly slipped across the table and over their entwined hands. Colt glanced up, and Sophia followed the direction of his gaze to see the waitress had arrived.

"I guess even the Broken Spur can have a little romance," she said as she placed glasses of ice water and two cups of coffee in front of them. "You two ready to order?"

Sophia felt like an idiot as she quickly pulled her hands away from Colt's and grabbed the menu. "Oh, I need another minute…if you don't mind."

"Sure, honey. Have a look while I take Mr. Scrooge's

order." She pulled a small notepad and short pencil from the back pocket of her jeans as she turned her attention to Colt.

Sophia quickly opened the menu where the evening special was written on a small scrap of paper clipped to the edge of folder. The offer of chili beans was all she needed to see before she placed the menu aside.

"Have you taken a look at your menu?" the waitress asked him. "Or do you only have eyes for your pretty date?"

"I don't need to look at the menu," he told the cheeky waitress. "Give me a chicken fried steak with a baked potato. And if you have any corn, can you add that to it?"

"Corn is on the special tonight with the chili beans, so I imagine I can talk the cook into giving you a spoonful." She arched a brow at Sophia. "Know what you want yet?"

If Sophia told the woman what she really wanted, the waitress's face would probably turn beet red. Or maybe it wouldn't, Sophia thought. According to Reeva, no matter how old a woman lived to be, she never forgot how it felt to have a man make love to her.

"I'll take the special," Sophia told her.

She scribbled the orders on her notepad. "Let me know if you need anything else."

After she'd walked away, Colt said with a wry

shake of his head, "You're ruining my reputation, Sophia. She thinks I'm Mr. Scrooge for bringing my date here to the Broken Spur for dinner."

"Your date? I didn't realize that's what I was to you," she said.

His expression turned sheepish. "Uh, what's wrong with calling you my date? We're out—together. And we like each other."

The simple explanation brought a smile to her face. "Yes, we do—like each other."

After their leisurely meal, they went to a small discount store where Sophia could pick up the items she needed, then on sudden impulse, Colt stopped by a liquor store to pick up a bottle of Holt's favorite whiskey.

By the time they returned to the ranch and parked in front of Reeva's house, the time was much later than Colt thought.

"It's getting late. You're going to hate me when the alarm goes off in the morning," he said, as he helped her down from the truck cab.

"I'll be fine when the alarm goes off," she assured him. "And being late isn't your fault. We're both guilty."

She reached inside the truck seat for her coat and Colt stepped up to help her pull it on. As he smoothed the fabric over her shoulders, the flowery scent of her perfume wafted up to him, and for one brief moment he thought about pulling her back against him and burying his face in her black hair.

Everything about her was so soft and feminine and lovely. And all through this evening, it had been a struggle to keep his focus on their conversation. Instead, he'd been picturing himself making love to her.

Making love. In his mind Colt had never considered the things that went on between a man and a woman in bed in that exact term. To him, it was *having sex.* He figured all men considered the act as such. Well, maybe Luke didn't, he thought. Because he loved Prudence so deeply. So why had Colt thought of it as making love tonight? He wasn't falling in love with Sophia. He was just a little charmed and infatuated with her. And those feelings would soon wane. That's why he needed to enjoy them now, he told himself.

"Would you like to come in for a bit? Gran will already be in bed. But her bedroom is on the far end of the house. We won't disturb her," she told him. "I'll make coffee. We didn't have dessert at the Broken Spur, and I'm sure Gran brought home some of the bread pudding she baked for the Hollisters. She cooked bourbon sauce to go with it, so it's beyond yummy."

She turned around and looked up at him, and Colt realized he couldn't have turned her down even if he knew walking through the front door was going to strike him blind.

"Sounds good to me," he told her. "I'll help you carry in your packages."

When they entered the house moments later, the living room was quiet with only the small glow of a night-light illuminating part of the area where a couch and two armchairs were grouped in a U shape.

Sophia gestured to one of the armchairs. "You can dump those bags into the armchair, and I'll deal with them later."

He placed the sacks down, then followed her through an open doorway and into a short hall that broke off into three sections.

"The kitchen is right in here," she told him, gesturing toward a slatted swinging door straight ahead of them. "I'll get the coffee going."

Trailing behind her, they entered the small room that was slightly illuminated with another night-light situated near a row of pine cabinets. Colt could see the walls were painted a sunny yellow, and a small round table was situated near a pair of double windows. The sheer white curtains were pulled to the sides and anchored with ties. Colt figured during the daylight hours, the view beyond the glass panes would be of the same creek that ran behind Luke and Prudence's house. The scenery would be mighty pretty, he thought. Especially with Sophia sitting at the table.

"Speaking of alarm clocks," she said, "when does yours go off in the mornings?"

He moved across the planked floor to where she was gathering the coffee makings.

"Usually around four thirty," he answered. "It depends on what's going on at the barn and the schedule that Holt has for the day. I try to be at work at five. What about you?"

"Gran and I are in the kitchen by four thirty. Not all the Hollisters eat breakfast at the same time. Chandler and Blake are usually the first, but not always. So we try to have everything ready to serve by five thirty," she told him.

"That makes for a long day," he said thoughtfully. "I'm betting the interior-design job you had was shorter hours."

"Not really. Most of the time I stayed up late at night, fretting over every little detail. I don't fret over my cooking." She gave him a playful smile. "Well, not much. Working with Gran is like having a safety net under me. You know what I mean?"

"Sure. Holt and Luke are mine."

"I really doubt you need a safety net, Colt."

He grunted with amusement. "I got you fooled. Now and then everyone needs someone to catch them when they fall. Including me."

"Gran says the same thing."

She poured water into the brewing machine and switched on the power. As Colt watched her going through the motions of making coffee, he could have told her that he didn't want coffee. He wanted her. But something held him back.

Hell. What was wrong with him, anyway? Sophia had given him plenty of signals that she liked him. And when they'd kissed last night in the barn, she'd made it clear that she'd enjoyed every second of being close to him. With any other woman, he would've already taken her to bed and satisfied his sexual urges. But that was the whole problem, he thought ruefully. With Sophia it was more than sex.

There you go again, Colt. You're already back to that sappy notion of making love. You need to snap out of it, boy. Sophia isn't an untouchable princess. She's a woman!

Drawing in a deep breath, he shoved at the mocking voice in his head and moved a step closer to her side. "You know, I'm still waiting to hear your thoughts on dinner at the Broken Spur," he said. "I'm beginning to think you were disappointed and didn't want to tell me."

Frowning with surprise, she turned to face him. "Oh, I thought I'd told you how much I enjoyed it!"

"No. You didn't."

"Sorry. I guess I expect you to read my mind."

Squinting, he leaned closer to her. "Let's see. If I peer into your forehead I'll spot a sign somewhere in your pretty head that reads *I liked everything about the Broken Spur.*"

"Right," she said with a soft laugh. "Anyway, I hope you'll want to go again sometime. It was such fun. I noticed everyone was eating like they were really enjoying the food. And our waitress mentioned that next week, in honor of the holiday, they'll start serving turkey and dressing on weekends. I'll bet it's scrumptious."

"Probably."

She frowned thoughtfully. "But then, Gran and I will be making gallons of it for the Hollisters' Christmas. I'll probably get my fill of it at the ranch house."

I hope you'll want to go again sometime.

Was she kidding? If he could manage it, he'd be happy to take her to the moon and back.

"A person can never have too much turkey and dressing," he told her.

The corners of her lips tilted to a provocative curve. "Hmm. You are reading my mind now. I'd better be careful. You might read something up there that…"

When she didn't go on, Colt dared to clasp a hand over her shoulder. "That matches my thoughts?"

The smile vanished from her lips as her gaze connected with his, and Colt wondered if some sort of magnetic field had formed in the scant space between them. Something was definitely drawing him toward her. Or was she the one inching closer to him?

Who or what was causing the invisible pull didn't matter, he decided. All that interested him was the soft light in her eyes and the gentle sigh rushing past her lips.

"I... What are you thinking, Colt?"

"That there's no way in heck I'll ever be able to leave this house without kissing you first."

Her lashes lowered, while her lips parted ever so slightly.

"I wouldn't think about letting you leave this house without kissing me," she murmured.

With those words she closed the last few inches between them and rested her palms in the middle of his chest. Feeling as if he were in some sort of dreamy fog, Colt slipped his arms around her waist and lowered his forehead to hers.

"I'm not sure this is right or good for either of us. But when I'm with you I morph into a man I don't recognize. All I want to do is touch you. Kiss you."

Her hands slipped upward until they were wrapped over the ridges of his shoulders. "Maybe it isn't good for us," she whispered, "but how will we ever know if we don't try to find out?"

"Sophia."

He angled his face downward until their breath was mingling, and then he slowly and gently touched his lips to hers. The kiss started out as a gentle exploration. But at some point, she took the lead, and before he realized what was happening, the kiss turned into a heated union with their tongues mating, their teeth nipping and teasing.

Heat boiled deep inside him, and before he could think or stop himself, his hands were on her buttocks, drawing her hips tightly to his burgeoning manhood. Even through the fabric of their clothing, he could feel the softness of her curves, the heat of her flesh. Like countless burning arrows, desire shot through him to leave his skin scorched and his senses swarming in all directions.

Somewhere among the rushing sounds in his head and the thought of carrying her to bed, he recognized she was groaning with need. Was it for him? Or did she need a chance to breathe?

It took superhuman effort to finally pull his mouth from hers, and even then his lips couldn't give up the taste of her skin. As he sucked in deep breaths, he continued to press them against her cheek and chin, then onto the side of her neck.

"Colt...oh...this is a little more than a kiss," she said, her voice thick with desire. "I didn't know it was...going to turn into...so much."

He knew he should ease the hold he had on her, but he couldn't. It felt so good and right to have their bodies pressed together. It was like nothing he could describe, except that she filled him with so many sweet emotions it was like his heart was going to overflow.

"Neither did I."

Using his lips, he traced lazy loops along her neck and back up to her cheek, but when he started to kiss her again, she suddenly turned her head and eased out of his arms.

Stunned, he stared at her. Was she going to give him a reason for the abrupt end to their embrace? Or did she consider pulling away from him explanation enough?

"I… Please don't look at me like that, Colt. I can't help it." With a choked sob, she turned her back to him and covered her face with her hands.

Totally confused by this instant change in her, Colt dared to place a hand on the back of her shoulder. "I don't understand what's wrong, Sophia. I thought you were… I thought that kiss was mutual. I admit it was getting out of hand, but I'd never do anything against your will."

"Oh, Colt, it's not that at all! You're so—" She whirled back to him, and as their gazes met, her eyes pleaded for understanding. "I want to be close to you. I mean, surely you could feel that! But I… guess I'm just not ready to jump into something…so serious. I mean, I don't know how you view things, but making love is serious to me."

Colt was surprised at just how much her words cut him. He'd never let a woman's rejection bother him before. There were too many of them out there willing to go to bed with him. Just because Sophia was backing away from him didn't mean the world was coming to an end.

But it sure as heck felt like it, he thought miserably.

"Is it something about me? You're thinking that I'm not what you need in your life right now?"

Shaking her head, she glanced to a spot across the room. "It's nothing like that. It's me. Since my engagement ended, I haven't had sex with anyone. To be honest, you're the only man that's managed to wake up that dead part of me. And I thought—no, that's wrong—I had hoped that when we kissed I'd want to keep going."

She'd not been with any man in more than a year. His thoughts whirled with that reality. What did it mean? That she'd loved the guy so much she couldn't bear to give herself to another man? For some reason that notion ripped him more than anything else.

"But you don't want to keep going," he said flatly.

She groaned. "I do. But I…"

Under normal circumstances, Colt would've already wished her well and walked out the door. Usually, he wouldn't consider wasting his time on an overly emotional, mixed-up woman. But Sophia wasn't just any woman. He didn't know how it had happened, but these past few days, he'd felt himself being drawn closer and closer to her. And it wasn't just a physical thing. Just being in her company, talking with her, hearing her voice and her laughter were sheer pleasure for him. He couldn't just walk away and pretend she didn't matter to him.

"You what?" he prompted.

Before he could guess her intentions, she reached for his hand. "Come with me, Colt. I want us to be sitting down when I tell you this."

Not knowing what to expect, he allowed her to lead him out to the semi-dark living room. Before they took a seat on the burgundy couch, he expected her to switch on a lamp to add to the glow of the night-light, but she didn't. Instead, she drew him down next to her on one of the wide cushions.

Before she said a word, he felt compelled to reassure her. "Listen, Sophia, you don't have to explain more than you already have. I get it. You're still a little hung up on your ex-fiancé. I can understand that. But that doesn't mean we have to stop enjoying each other's company. We can have dates without getting... physical."

It would be as hard as hell not to kiss or hold her, but he could do it. He could do anything, except give her up completely.

She let out a long sigh, then folded her hands together atop her lap. "I do have to explain, Colt. I think I need to—for my sake and yours."

"As long as it's what you want."

"It is," she said, then sighing, she turned her gaze away from him and out at the darkened room. "When I told you about my engagement, I didn't tell you exactly why it ended."

"From what you said, I assumed the man was so consumed with his job he didn't have time for you."

"That's only a part of it. True, he was immersed in his job with the firm. The more cases he won, the more likely he would move up the corporate ladder. And his goal had always been to reach the very top." She turned a rueful look to him. "But I knew that much about him when we met. I thought I could deal with it. After all, he was hardworking and successful, and most of us have careers that we have to juggle with our personal lives. I reasoned that if Tristen could adjust to the hours I put into my job, then I could surely put up with his. And for the most part we handled that issue."

"Then, what happened? You discovered he was cheating on you?"

She grimaced. "He was the type who would've told me he wanted to have an affair before he ever allowed that to happen. No, we had…you see, when we first started dating, he'd made it clear that he didn't want children. At least, not right away. I was agreeable to that. We were both caught up in our careers, and I could see that we needed time to establish a home and a married life before we became parents. But in spite of me using birth control, I somehow ended up pregnant."

His throat was suddenly thick, and he cleared it in the hope that when he did finally speak, he wouldn't sound like he'd swallowed a frog.

"Let me guess. This Tristen guy wasn't happy when you told him about the baby."

She let out a bitter snort. "Livid is more like it. He accused me of deliberately getting pregnant. He reminded me over and over that he'd made it clear from the start that he didn't want children. Yet I went against his wishes anyway. At first I tried to defend myself and insisted I would never do anything so deceptive. But then as I listened to him spewing such hate at me, I decided defending myself to him was stupid. I shouldn't have to defend myself for a situation that was hardly my own doing."

Colt frowned. "Lawyers are supposed to be smart. This jerk sounds as dumb as a rock. Any man with an ounce of sense knows that, aside from abstinence, foolproof birth control doesn't exist. A man of any caliber would've gladly owned up to his responsibility. Hell, he should've been thrilled."

I would've been.

From out of nowhere the thought jolted through him like a loud crack of thunder. Up until this moment, he'd never really given much thought about finding a woman and having children. Oh, there had been times when he'd watched Luke with little J.J. and wondered how it would feel to have a child. But he'd never actually planned to make that a goal in life.

"Thrilled? Oh, Colt. Tristen revealed the kind of

man he truly was, and the revelation was ugly. He admitted that he'd lied all along about eventually wanting kids. He'd only told me that to pacify me until we were married. And as far as the baby I was carrying, he wanted nothing to do with it. He gave me an ultimatum. Him or the baby. And dear God, that had been the easiest choice I'd ever had to make. I handed the engagement ring to him, along with the prediction that someday he'd end up crawling on his belly—all snakes did."

"Smart girl. Only he deserved more than that. He needed a good right hook." He reached for her hand and pressed it between his. "It's obvious you didn't have the baby. What happened?"

Her head dropped, and as silence began to stretch to an uncomfortable length, he decided she wasn't going to tell him. And she had that right, he thought. But he wanted to think she trusted him enough to share that intimate part of her past.

Finally, she said, "I suffered a miscarriage in my fourth month. Why, I don't know. The doctor couldn't give me a definite reason. Other than it wasn't meant to be. But it hurt. It still hurts. And now…when we were kissing so passionately a few minutes ago, it all came rushing back to me. I'm afraid, Colt. The thought of getting involved with another man and taking the chance of getting pregnant leaves me in a cold sweat. What if the relationship didn't work out—or I had another miscarriage? I'm not sure if I could bear that much pain again."

She looked up at him, and he braced himself to deal with a waterfall of tears. Instead the beautiful brown orbs were as dry and bleak as a stretch of desert sand.

She said, "I used such bad judgment when I got involved with Tristen. I'm not sure I can trust myself to make the right choices the next time around. And now you're probably thinking I'm a weak person. That I need to find some courage."

Her voice was strained and wobbly, and Colt ached to pull her into his arms and comfort her. But after all she'd just told him, he wasn't sure if she would welcome being in his arms.

"I'll tell you what I think, Sophia. You're a very strong woman. And I'm glad you came to Three Rivers."

And to me.

The thought running through his head very nearly rolled off his tongue. But at the last second, he managed to bite it back. She might get the idea he was falling headfirst for her and that would be misleading. He wasn't falling. He was just caring—a little too much.

She squeezed his hand, and then with a muffled cry, she threw her arms around him and buried her face in the side of his neck.

The unexpected reaction caught him off guard,

but after a moment's hesitation, he gently wrapped his arms around her and snugged her close to his chest.

"I'm very glad, too, Colt. Glad that I found you." She eased her head back and locked her gaze on his. "I only hope you won't give up on me. And you'll give us a chance to—get to know each other better."

He touched his fingertips to her cheek. "Why would I give up on you?"

Her eyes blinked, and he prayed she wasn't going to cry. He didn't think he could bear to see her tears.

"Because I-I'm carrying around so many emotional scars and hang-ups from the past. And I need time to find the strength and the courage to push them aside and move on. Most guys don't want to waste their time waiting around for a woman like me to deal with her problems."

He gave her a lopsided grin. "I'm not just any guy, Sophia."

She smiled then, and as his gaze roamed her sweet face, he realized just how much her happiness meant to him.

"No," she said softly. "You're not just any guy."

His focus fell to her lips, and the urge to kiss her struck him hard, but he managed to summon up enough strength to push it aside.

"I imagine that coffee is done by now, don't you?" he asked. "I think I heard two bowls of bread pudding calling our name."

Still smiling, she eased off the couch and reached for his hand. And as Colt followed her into the kitchen, he wondered if he was a fool to think he was man enough to make her want to love again.

Chapter Eight

"Are you going to be coming back home for Christmas? Dozens of parties are already scheduled before the big day, and naturally Richard is throwing the biggest one. I understand the two of you didn't part on the best of terms, but I also know he'd be thrilled to see you. To have you back in the company, too."

From her seat beneath the covered patio, Sophia glanced across the busy ranch yard to where the horse barn was situated among a group of pens and smaller barns. Two days had passed since she and Colt had eaten at the Broken Spur and she'd ended up telling him about the baby and the subsequent breakup with Tristen. She'd not seen or talked to him since he'd left her grandmother's house that night, and she was beginning to wonder if revealing her scarred baggage had put him off.

"Sophia? Are you there? Or am I talking to a dead phone connection?"

Shaking away her troubled thoughts, Sophia adjusted the cell phone against her ear and tried to focus on her friend's voice.

"I'm here, Fallon, and I'm not the least bit interested in returning to California or my old job. And I wouldn't mind a bit if you told Richard that. Now I really need to get back to the kitchen. My grandmother is putting meatballs together, and I'm to do all the browning."

The other woman groaned, and Sophia could easily picture her rolling her eyes and tossing her long lilac-colored hair over one shoulder. Fallon was an assistant at West Coast Designs where Sophia had worked and the two women had been friends since their high-school days together, but they were as different as night and day.

"Oh, Sophia, you need your head examined. How can you stand being cooped up in a kitchen, smelling grease and chopping food and mixing up dough? I'd be running and screaming to the nearest psychiatrist's couch!"

"That's why you're there and I'm here. And to answer your earlier question, I'm already home, Fallon. I've no intentions of flying out to California for Christmas or any other reason."

Fallon sputtered. "But what about your mom? Aren't you planning on spending the holiday with her?"

"No. She'll have plenty of her friends over to keep her company. You know, the snobs who pretend to have money but in reality are financially on the rocks. Mom enjoys those types of people. I don't. And anyway, I wouldn't leave Gran for all the gold in the state of Arizona."

Nor did she want to miss the chance of spending at least part of the holiday with Colt. Maybe she was hoping for too much. Especially after the way she'd put a chill on their physical contact. But he'd told her he wasn't going to hold that against her, and she had to believe he was being truthful.

Yeah, sure, Sophia. Like Tristen was truthful. He only told you what he believed you wanted to hear. And that's all Colt is doing. Pacifying you with words that mean little to him.

"So I'm supposed to believe that you're happy out there in Arizona?" her friend asked.

Fallon's question interrupted the sarcastic voice in Sophia's head, and she rubbed her fingers against her forehead as if the tiny massage would keep the dismal thoughts away.

"I'm very happy here in Arizona, Fallon. I know

that's hard for you to understand. You and I want different things in life. And what I want is here."

After a moment, Fallon said, "Okay, I'll try to accept that. Can I assume you've met a man?"

Sophia squeezed the phone a tad tighter. "You can assume all you want to."

Fallon chuckled slyly. "I recognize that tone in your voice. You're trying to hide something. Which means you have met a man."

"Could be. But it's…nothing serious."

"Where you and men are concerned, it has to be serious. You're one of those old-fashioned girls who believe love equals marriage. Whereas I think men equal fun and that's all. Period."

Sophia did her best not to groan. "Hmm. Well, I'll admit it, Fallon, I'd be much better off if I could follow your rule book on men. But it's just not my style. And anyway, after that fiasco with Tristen, I'm not sure I'll ever trust my judgment in men."

"I'll admit he had that cute, preppy look. But he was as boring as plain wallpaper. By the way, I saw him the other day in the coffee shop on the corner. He looked like hell and not like himself at all. That ought to make you happy."

"What makes me happy is that I felt nothing when you mentioned seeing him. But as far as me wanting someone to suffer, that's not me. I wouldn't wish that on my worst enemy. If I did, I'd be putting myself in Tristen's league."

"No. You're not vengeful like I am," she said with a devilish laugh. "But that's enough about your ex-fiancé."

"Beyond enough. So tell me what you've been doing," Sophia said.

"At work or play?" she asked, then giggled. "The latter is more interesting."

"I'm sure."

Sophia listened to her friend's stories for a couple more minutes before she finally ended the call and returned to the kitchen.

Reeva had already filled one pan with meatballs and was starting on another.

"Sorry, Gran. I'll get these started right now. I couldn't get off the phone." She reached for the bib apron she'd taken off during her short break on the patio and slipped it over her head. "Sometimes I wish Fallon wouldn't call me. When I tell her I have no intention of going back to California she thinks I'm joking."

"I imagine this kind of life sounds boring to your friend," Reeva remarked. "Especially if she's a young person."

"She's my age. We went through all four years of high school together. And then later, we ended up working for the same company. I like her a lot, but I'm not so sure you would, Gran. She wears extremely flamboyant clothes and her hair is—well,

I'll just say it looks unusual. But she's good-hearted. Sometimes too much."

Reeva continued shaping a portion of seasoned ground meat into a ball. "A person's appearance doesn't always tell you who or what they really are, Sophia. If you take a good look at all the old western movies, you'll notice the villains were usually dressed in suits and ties. And the good guys in plain work clothes."

Sophia switched the fire on beneath a huge iron skillet. "Why do you think it was that way?"

"Because the suits looked smooth and respectable on the outside and hid the deception and corruption beneath. The plain clothes represented simple, hard-working folks. I think it's an image that dates back to the Great Depression. But it still fits today. Anyway, you can't judge a bird by its feathers. Eagle or sparrow, they're all just birds. It's up to us to figure out if they're a predator or prey. I'm fairly certain your friend must be a nice person. Otherwise, she wouldn't be your friend."

As Sophia oversaw the browning of the meatballs, she couldn't help thinking how she'd made that very mistake with Tristen. He'd been perfectly groomed on the outside with designer suits and ties and expensive shoes on his feet. The showy feathers had hidden the rotten core beneath. And unfortunately she hadn't uncovered it until she'd already been drawn into his life. But Colt was different. His denim jeans and shirts were usually covered with dust, the soles of his boots caked with dirt and horse manure.

Did that make him true through and through? Did that mean he might not break her heart, too? Not exactly, she thought. There were plenty of guys wearing suits that were good men, and just as many wearing jeans who were bad. But so far Colt had been far more genuine than any man she'd known. And dangerous or not, she couldn't put him, or his kisses, out of her mind.

Sophia and Reeva wound up their kitchen duties earlier than usual, but it was still well past dark when they left the ranch house and headed home. As Sophia drove the truck over the bumpy dirt road, she tried not to feel a little dejected. She'd been hoping Colt might stop by the kitchen and say hello or at least send her a friendly text. But he'd done neither. Now as she drove the old work truck in the direction of the river, she had to face the fact that another day was going to pass without any contact from him.

"You've been kinda quiet, honey," Reeva remarked when Sophia parked the truck in front of the house. "Are you feeling okay?"

"I'm fine, Gran. Just doing some thinking."

"Good. Because I need you to do something for me in a little while."

In spite of Reeva taking plenty of breaks throughout the day, Sophia figured her grandmother was tired by the time evening finally arrived.

"Do what? Make coffee so you can prop up your feet and enjoy a cup in front of the television?"

Reeva swatted a hand through the air as she climbed out of the truck cab. "I'd rather use my time staring at an anthill than at the TV screen. The ants would be a heck of a lot more entertaining."

Sophia wanted to laugh as she followed Reeva into the house. But since her grandmother was being serious, she stifled her amusement. "Okay. Then what do you want me to do?"

"Help me get the Christmas decorations down from the attic. I can do it. But why should I when you're young and spry and can climb the ladder a whole lot better than me?"

Sophia shut the door behind them. "Gran, why bother with the decorations tonight? There's no use in pulling all those boxes out until we get a tree. If you're that anxious, I'll drive into town tonight and buy one. I noticed the grocery store has a few."

"No, no. I don't want you to do that." She made a shooing gesture toward the hallway. "Go on and change out of your cooking clothes. We'll talk about getting a tree after you get comfortable."

Sophia went to her bedroom and changed into a pair of loose jeans and a soft white sweater she wore for lounging around the house. After slipping on a pair of leather flats, she let down her hair from the ballerina bun she wore while working and brushed the black waves loose upon her shoulders.

She was headed back down the hallway to the front of the house when she heard a knock on the door and then her grandmother's voice calling to her.

"Sophia, come here. We have company."

Company? As long as she'd been living here, they'd never had company!

She walked to the living room and then stopped in her tracks as she saw Reeva standing to one side, watching Colt lug a huge Christmas tree through the front door.

Sophia rushed forward a few steps, then stopped and stared at the two of them. "What's going on?"

Reeva's expression was like a cat who'd just discovered a saucer of cream. "This is why I didn't want you going after a tree. I knew Colt would drive up any minute with one."

Sophia's gaze traveled from Reeva to where Colt was still maneuvering the spruce through the door opening.

"If you knew he was bringing a tree, why didn't you tell me?" she asked her grandmother.

Reeva continued to look uncommonly smug, and Sophia could only wonder what her grandmother had been secretly planning behind her back.

"Colt wanted to surprise you," Reeva said. "And if you're thinking I've been meddling, just stop it. This was all his idea."

By now Colt had managed to wedge the last of the branches through the door. After he'd closed it behind him, he turned and beamed a broad smile at Sophia.

"You are surprised, aren't you?" he asked.

Just the sight of him and that oh-so-sexy smile was enough to melt her right where she stood. "*Surprised* is putting it mildly. Where did you get the tree?"

"Maurcen and Gil purchased a truckload of trees up at Prescott and hauled them down here to the ranch. I managed to stake my claim on one of them before they were all snatched up."

And he'd taken the time and trouble to surprise her with it. She tried to tell herself that the gesture wasn't that big a deal. But it was. So big, in fact, that she hardly knew how to react.

Slowly, she walked over and touched a sprig on the blue spruce. "It's lovely, Colt. And the smell is heavenly. Look, Gran, isn't it the most beautiful trce?"

"It's a dandy," Reeva agreed. "And tall. Reckon it will fit without the top bending over at the ceiling?"

"I'll trim off the bottom if need be. I have a hand-saw in the truck," Colt told her.

He walked to the center of the room and made a quick survey of the space. "Where do you ladies want the tree set up? In front of the windows? In a corner?"

Reeva said, "You choose, Sophia. This is your first Christmas on the ranch. I want it to be special for you."

This was the first and only holiday she'd ever spent with her grandmother, and for that reason alone it was going to be special. Not to mention having Colt be a part of their celebration.

Sophia moved across the room to give Reeva a tight hug. "Oh, Gran, I'm with you. And I love you. For me, that makes it the best Christmas ever."

Reeva gently patted her shoulder and then promptly set her aside. "Sophia, I'm going to be angry if you make me cry and embarrass Colt with all this mush."

"Okay, Gran, I'll quit all the mush." She pecked a little kiss on her grandmother's cheek, then stepping aside, she focused on finding the best spot to put the tree. After a moment, she walked over to the set of double windows. "This should be perfect. The twinkling lights will shine through the windows and make it easy for Santa to see our house. We don't want him to pass us by," she added with a teasing grin.

Colt shook a playful finger at her. "It's not the lights that will have him stopping. It's whether you've been naughty or nice. That's the warning my brother keeps giving me."

She shot him a wicked grin. "For your information, I'm the picture of niceness. And Gran's even nicer than me!"

Snorting, Reeva started out of the room. "You two get to work with the tree. I need a cup of coffee."

She left for the kitchen, and Sophia walked over to where Colt was standing by the tree.

Now that the two of them were alone, she felt a little awkward. For the past two days she'd relived their red-hot kiss and then her breaking down like a frightened and inexperienced schoolgirl. She'd been fearing that she'd ruined everything with him. But here he was, and it was all she could do not to throw her arms around him.

"I'm happy to see you, Colt. I was beginning to think you'd erased me from your girlfriend list."

His lips twisted into a wry grin. "You're the only girl on my list. If I erased your name, all I'd have is a blank page."

"Where did you learn that cheesy line?" she teased.

With his forefinger, he made an imaginary X over his heart. "I can't help how it sounds. It's the truth."

"Well, since we're being honest and I'm not worrying about sounding corny, my page is blank, too. Except for your name," she added.

He reached out and lightly curled his hand around her upper arm. "I started to text you and then I thought you might appreciate a little break from me. But I've missed you," he said. "The past two nights

I've been extra busy at the barn, so I ended up eating with the bunkhouse boys. And that's not anything like eating dinner with you."

His words swelled her heart with joy. "I've missed you, too. And I'm glad you're not annoyed with me."

Frowning, he stepped closer and lowered his voice. "Why would I be annoyed? I'm glad you told me everything about…what you went through. It helps me understand a lot of things about you—and me. Now we can start over, and this time we'll be on safer footing. Right?"

She didn't know about being safer, but she definitely wanted to start over with him. "Right."

His gaze continued to hold hers, and while she studied the dark, dark depths of his eyes, she was acutely aware of his hand on her arm and how the warmth from it was spreading throughout her body. How did she think she could remain in his presence and not end up making love to him? She'd have to be superhuman to resist the fire he built in her.

Ever since Sophia's engagement had ended, she'd had no urge to have a physical relationship with another man. Tristen's betrayal and the subsequent loss of the baby had turned off all her sexual desires. She'd even begun to fear she might never want to make love again. Until she'd met Colt and suddenly she'd started to feel and want again.

Maybe it wouldn't be so dangerous to let herself make love to Colt, she contemplated. She could see he was a far more caring and selfless man than Tristen. Maybe it was time she started trusting her judgment and trusting Colt.

He must have been reading her thoughts or was experiencing a mental tussle of his own, because he suddenly dropped his hand and stepped back from her.

"Well…uh…we'd better get to work, or Reeva's going to come back in here and find the tree still on the floor," he said.

Giving herself a mental shake, she said, "We don't want that to happen. Let's get started. Did you happen to bring a tree stand with you? If not, I'll see if Gran has one."

"No worries. I have one in the truck."

He left the house to fetch the stand, and once he returned they went to work erecting the spruce in front of the double windows.

When they finally had the tree standing upright, Colt stood back to survey it. "Looks straight and sturdy to me. Do you want me to trim any of the branches?"

"Thanks for offering. But I want it to look natural. Like it just came out of the forest."

Smiling indulgently, he said, "I think this tree did come straight out of the forest and right to your house. Now, about the decorations. You said something about getting in the attic?"

"Yes, but maybe we need to check with Gran before we get those. She was planning on popcorn and cranberry garlands. And—"

"Sorry, Sophia. With our schedules being so busy I don't have time for making those," Reeva interrupted as she walked into the room. "I didn't learn until this morning that Colt was going to bring the tree. And there's nothing more depressing to me than an undecorated tree."

Colt said, "My bad. I should've given you a heads-up before this morning. But I didn't learn until last night that Maureen and Gil were going after the trees."

"Oh my gosh, Colt, don't apologize! The tree is the important thing," Sophia told him. "The garland is no big deal. Whatever we find in the attic will be perfect."

"I'm sure you'll find a few strings of lights and some glass balls up there," Reeva said. "And seems like I had a box of icicles left over from last year. You might find more if you dig through all the boxes."

"I'll dig," Sophia assured her, then motioned for Colt to follow her into the hallway. "If you'll pull the ladder down for me, I'll go searching."

She showed him the handle pull in the ceiling and flipped a switch on the wall that controlled a light in the attic. When he pulled down the wooden ladder, he said, "I can't let you go searching alone. I'll be right behind you."

As they climbed toward the open square in the

ceiling, Reeva said, "There's a wooden trunk up there, too, Sophia. If you care to look, you might find a few decorations in it."

"I will, Gran. Thanks," Sophia called down to her. "And don't worry. Everything we find that we think we can use, we'll haul down."

Sophia finished her climb into the attic, then moved to one side of the opening to give Colt plenty of room to lever himself into the storage space.

"Heat definitely rises," she said as she glanced around at the cluttered space. "It's far warmer up here than the lower part of the house. If Three Rivers is ever hit by a blizzard, I'll know where to come to warm up."

"If a person needed to thaw out, this is definitely the place," Colt agreed. "But the ceiling is not quite tall enough for a hat."

He removed his Stetson and laid it on the nearest flat object he could find, then bending at the waist, followed Sophia through a maze of old furniture pieces and other household items.

"Most of this stuff needs to be chucked into a junk pile rather than stored away. I hope dust doesn't make you sneeze," she said as she eyed an old pleated lampshade. "Everything is coated with it."

He chuckled. "Sophia, I eat dust all day long out in the training pen. If it made me sneeze I'd be in big trouble."

She groaned at her mistake. "In my defense, I'll

say there are many different types of dust. But honestly, I wasn't thinking about the flying dirt you deal with on your job. Before I moved here I'd only made a few visits to Three Rivers, and those visits were short. Until recently I was never around men who worked outdoors for their livelihood. It's taking some getting used to. Everything is different. But different in a nice way," she added.

"Well, I never had a girlfriend who cooked for a living. So we're even on that score."

There he was calling her his girlfriend again, she thought. He couldn't possibly know what hearing that did to her. It filled her with a warm and wanted feeling. Like coming home after a long, exhausting journey.

She laughed. "You'll get used to me reeking of frying oil and burnt coffee."

"And you'll grow accustomed to me stinking of dust and horse manure. We make a fine-smelling pair," he said jokingly.

Pausing to get her bearings, she glanced around the shadowy area. "Gran told me the decorations were at the east end of the attic. Is that the direction we're headed?"

"Yes. Do you need an extra light? If you want I'll switch on the flashlight on my phone."

"Light is not the problem. There's just so much junk up here. Looks like years of it." She'd barely gotten the words out when she spotted two large cardboard boxes with the word *Christmas* written in black marker on the sides. "Oh! There it is, Colt. Let's have a look!"

They made their way to the boxes, and Colt pulled the first one out in the narrow walk space and opened the lid.

"I see strands of lights in this one," he said. "Let's have a look in the other."

The next box contained shiny balls of red, green and gold. There was also an angel with feathery white wings and long dark hair that was slightly tangled in the halo attached to her head.

"Oh, an angel!" Kneeling in front of the box, Sophia picked up the delicate angel and gently used the tip of her forefinger to smooth her hair into place. "I can't wait to see how beautiful she'll look at the top of the tree!"

Realizing she sounded like a little child, she looked up at him. "Sorry. For a minute there I thought I was eight years old again."

"Don't be sorry for that. It's good to be a kid at heart sometimes. Especially at Christmas." Squatting at her side, he studied the angel. "Her robe is a little wrinkled. But she does look magical. Like you."

He'd spoken the last two words very softly, and she looked around to see he was gazing straight at her face, rather than the angel in her hands. The look in his eyes caused her heart to squeeze with longing.

She desperately wished she was brave enough

to throw her fears and inhibitions aside. To give herself to this man without worrying about the future. Maybe eventually she could be that woman. Right now she had to hope he'd give her the time she needed to find her courage.

"Thank you, Colt. That's sweet of you."

His gaze swept over her face, and then his fingers gently brushed through the hair resting on her shoulder.

"Did you know I've memorized your face?" he murmured. "I remember every little curve and dip, the length of your straight little nose and the tiny hollow between it and your lips. Your eyes are a jumbled shade of browns, and your lashes are too long to be real. But I can see that they are real. Just like your smile. And that's the most beautiful thing about you. We've not known each other for that long and this is happening so fast for me. But I don't care. I know how I feel when I hold you."

By the time his words died away, Sophia's throat was thick with unshed tears. "Are you trying to make me cry?" she asked in a hoarse voice.

"No. I just want you to know that when I look at you, it's like a Christmas homecoming to me."

"And when I look at you, I feel happy. That's sort of the same thing, isn't it?"

"Happy, yes."

She cleared her throat and rose to her full height. "Let's see if we can find the trunk."

"It's over there," Colt said. "By the iron bedstead."

They worked their way through a stack of plastic bins and a pile of galvanized buckets and washtubs until they eventually reached the trunk. The frame was made of wood with the top covered in some sort of red fabric that had faded and partially disintegrated.

"This trunk doesn't look like anyone has opened it in years," Sophia said. "I can't imagine Gran having stored decorations in it. Maybe her memory is confused."

"Well, it won't take long to find out," Colt said.

He unfastened the latch, and the rusty hinges squeaked as he lifted open the lid and rested it against the wall.

Most of the things inside were wrapped in pillowcases or towels, and the faint scent of lavender sachets lingered on the linens as Sophia began to slowly search through the odd assortment of items. There were pieces of old clothing that must have held a sentimental value to her grandmother. Most of them were carefully folded and stacked neatly in one corner, along with a pair of white pumps with tiny black bows on the toes.

"Size seven. These had to have been Gran's. Wonder when she wore them?"

"Maybe when she got married," Colt suggested.

Sophia took another look at the shoe, but this time

the footwear took on a different meaning. "Aww. Do you think so?"

"Some women like to keep those sorts of things. You should know."

No. She'd never had a chance to wear a wedding dress or press a flower from her bridal bouquet, Sophia thought dismally. She had no keepsakes. Only bitter memories of a marriage and baby that never came to be.

She looked down at the shoe, then over to him. "Did your mother keep her wedding things?"

He nodded. "She was the kind who'd keep a gum wrapper if it held some sort of meaning for her. Dad still has all her things. He never looks at them. But sometimes Luke and I do, just to think back and remember. It's bittersweet, you know?"

"Yes. I do." Not wanting to choke up again, she focused on prowling through the contents in the trunk. Eventually, she began to find a few homemade ornaments that must have been stored from years past.

"Oh my, I wasn't expecting to find anything like this." Sophia held up a bell that had been carved from a piece of soft wood. "Look, Colt. It says *Merry Christmas to my wife 1966*. My grandfather must have made this for Gran. Before he...went off to war. It must have been their last Christmas together. Do you think it would upset her if we hung it on the tree?"

"No. It won't upset her," he said. "She told you

to look in the trunk for ornaments. And I have the feeling that she hadn't forgotten anything in here."

Sophia sighed. "She must have been thinking now was a good time for me to see these things."

"Probably."

She placed the wooden bell on a hand towel, then lifted a few more ornaments from the trunk. Some were made of wood and others shiny metal. Sophia placed them alongside the bell and was about to tell Colt to shut the lid, when she noticed a framed picture beneath a stack of vinyl 45 rpm records.

Easing it from beneath the records, she found herself gazing at the image of a very young Reeva holding her one and only child. Reeva's hair was black and wavy, and beneath an A-line minidress her figure was a bit fuller and curvier than now. She was smiling at the camera, and Sophia supposed at that time in her life, Reeva had no idea that the baby girl in her arms would eventually disown her.

"Oh God, I wish I hadn't seen this," she said, her voice husky.

He reached over and took the photo from her hands. "Why? This is your grandmother, isn't it? She was a real looker back then."

"Yes, and that makes it even sadder. At this time she was already a widow. And the baby in her arms is my mother. I look at this and there's so many emotions…" A hot lump was suddenly choking off the remainder of her words, and she quickly bent her head and tried to swallow it away.

Colt's hand came to rest on her shoulder. "Are you okay?"

Her eyes were full of tears, and she dashed them aside with the back of her hand before she looked at him. "Forgive me, Colt. I'm not normally so emotional. I got to thinking…about too many things."

"Dealing with the chasm between your mother and grandmother can't be easy. But you have your own life to live, Sophia. Someday you'll have a family of your own, and you can feel good in knowing you'll be a different mother. You'll be kind, loving and forgiving."

Her tear-glazed eyes focused on his face. "Do you honestly see me that way?"

"I do."

Her lips quivered as she gave him a grateful smile. "Thank you. And please don't tell Reeva I got weepy over this photo. She wouldn't like it. She wants me to be happy."

He touched a finger to the tip of her nose. "I want you to be happy, too. So let's gather everything together and carry it down to the living room. What do you say?"

She cupped her hand against the side of his face. "I say I'm glad that you're here with me."

Drawing her hand away from his cheek, he placed

a kiss in the middle of her palm, then gently tugged her to her feet.

"Come on. We have work to do."

The night was growing late by the time the tree was decorated and the three of them sat in the living room finishing the last of the pumpkin bread and coffee that Reeva had prepared for a snack.

"The tree is ready for a visit from Santa, and there's not a crumb of pumpkin bread left. Thank you, ladies, for a great evening, but I need to head home."

Rising from his seat in the couch, he levered on his hat and reached for the jacket lying across the back of a nearby chair.

"And I need to be heading to bed," Reeva announced as she also rose to her feet. "Sophia, you show Colt out."

"Yes, Gran. And leave the dishes. I'll take care of everything," she said.

While Reeva left the room, Sophia pulled on a denim jacket and coiled a scarf around her neck.

"You really don't need to see me out," Colt said as she joined him at the front door. "It's not like I can't find my truck."

"But I want to walk you out," she insisted. "It's the least I can do after all you've done for me and Gran tonight."

With his hand on the doorknob, he paused and

took one last look at the tree. "I think Reeva was really touched that we used the ornaments your grandfather had given her."

"It takes a lot to make Gran smile. But she did. That tells me how touched she was."

He opened the door and stepped out into the cold night. Sophia followed and quickly shut the door behind them.

As they walked in the direction of his truck, she reached for his hand, and as Colt wrapped his fingers around hers, he decided he'd never had any woman give him so many mixed signals. At times she looked at him as though she wanted to fall into his arms and repeat the scorching kiss they'd experienced the other evening. Then other times, she seemed wary and even shy about being close to him. He didn't know what to expect from her.

Still, he continued to remind himself that their relationship had developed at a rapid pace and caught both of them by surprise. She'd told him that she needed time to deal with the mistakes she'd made with her ex-fiancé and Colt could also see how the loss of the baby had cut her deeply. The whole regrettable experience had skewered her ability to trust her own judgment. And if she couldn't trust herself, how could he ever expect her to trust him?

He didn't have the answer to that question. He only knew that if it took him from now to doomsday, he was going to convince her that they were right for each other.

"Have you heard that Joe and Tessa are going to have a big Christmas party and barn dance next Saturday?" she asked. "Jazelle told me about it this morning. Besides family, all the Three River hands are being invited, along with those who work the Bar X."

He said, "I haven't heard about this. But I'm sure once the guys find out, they'll be bursting to spread the news."

She glanced up at him. "Since I've moved here, I've not had a chance to go to a ranch party yet, so I'm excited. Will you be going?"

"Oh, well, I think I could be talked into it if the right girl asked me to go," he said with a clever grin.

She pulled a playful face at him. "I thought cowboys were traditional guys. Aren't you supposed to be inviting me?"

Laughing, he tugged her toward him and held her in the loose circle of his arms. "Miss Vandale, would you do the honor of accompanying me to the Christmas dance?"

Was that twinkle in her eyes brought on by the starlight or from being in his arms? Either way, it was a mighty struggle for Colt not to bend his head and put his lips on hers.

"It would be my pleasure, Mr. Crawford."

"Great," he said with a smile, then dropping his

hold on her, he turned and opened the door to the truck. "In the meantime, I'd better get going."

Just as he started to climb beneath the steering wheel, he felt her hand touch his shoulder, and he turned a questioning look at her.

"I just wanted to say thank you—again. And good-night."

Did she have any idea what she was doing to him? How much he wanted to grab her up and smother her with so many kisses she wouldn't be able to remember the pain of her past?

"Good night, Sophia."

His gaze held hers for long moments, and then she suddenly stood on tiptoes and pressed her lips to his.

The kiss was soft and so achingly sweet it twisted his stomach into hungry knots. And once it was over, he didn't trust himself to linger in her company for another minute. He quickly climbed into the truck and, lifting his hand in a final farewell, drove away.

Chapter Nine

Minutes later, Colt was nearing a junction in the dirt road when his lingering thoughts of Sophia were suddenly interrupted by the ring of his cell phone.

Wondering who might be calling at this late hour, he pulled out the phone, half expecting it to be Sophia, and was a bit uneasy to see the call was from Holt.

Pulling over to the side of the road and braking the truck to a stop, he answered on the second ring. "What's up?"

"I know it's late and you're probably already settled in for the night, but I need some help with Bluebonnet."

Colt frowned as he pictured the blue roan mare. They weren't expecting her baby to arrive for another two weeks. "She's trying to foal?"

"Yes. She's been in labor for a while now, but nothing is happening. Damn it, Chandler's not home. He's out on an emergency call."

"Hang on. I'm here at the road junction. I'll be there in five minutes."

He hung up the phone and stomped on the gas.

When he reached the horse barn, he trotted inside, then, not wanting to spook any of the stalled horses, he eased down to long, hurried strides toward the foaling area. Halfway there, Farley, the groom that Colt had left on barn watch tonight, intercepted him. The worried look on his face spoke volumes.

"Bluebonnet isn't in the foaling area. She's still in her stall," he told Colt in a rushed voice. "She was already down when I found her. And I was making ten-minute rounds. Holt says she's early. But I feel bad—I should've been making five-minute rounds."

As the two men strode rapidly down the aisle of the barn, Colt frowned at the groom. "Damn it, Farley, quit beating yourself up. You've already had a hard day. You can't spend the whole night continuously walking! Just pray that Bluebonnet and the foal will be okay. That's all you need to do."

"I've already done that," Farley said.

"Then you need to quit worrying."

At Bluebonnet's stall the two men found Holt

squatted on his heels and stroking the mare's sides. Colt quickly entered the twelve-by-twelve-foot space.

"What do you think might be going on with her?"

"I'm not sure. This is her second foal. She didn't have any trouble with the first one."

"Her flanks are drawn and damp. She's definitely in pain." He looked thoughtfully at Holt. "Has her water broken?"

"No," Holt answered. "Unless something happened before Farley found her. But I don't believe it has."

"Could be her bag is too thick to break." Squatting over the mare, he gently moved her tail aside for a closer look. "I don't see the placenta yet. Could be she's going to have a red bag birth. If so, we'll need a sharp scalpel to cut through the bag. Otherwise, the foal will die from lack of oxygen."

"Yeah, red bag has been going through my mind, too." Holt glanced up at Farley who was hovering anxiously at the gate of the stall. "Go get the medical bag out of the foaling room. Pronto!"

Nodding, Farley took off, and Holt moved over to where Colt was still squatted at the mare's back end. "Have you ever done the procedure?" he asked.

Colt said, "A couple of times. And only because my boss forced me to. He said it was something every horseman needs to know."

"Thank God your old boss saw to it that you got the experience. I've watched Chandler do the procedure, but with a vet on scene there was never any need for me to attempt it. Think you can manage the task—if it comes to that?"

Lifting his hat from his head, Colt raked a hand through his hair. The foals at Three Rivers Ranch weren't just run-of-the-mill. They were worth a stack of money, even before they were born. If Colt messed up and caused the foal or the mother to die, it would be more than emotional devastation for him and the family. It would mean a huge financial loss for the ranch.

"If it comes to that, there won't be any time to wonder," Colt told him with far more confidence than he felt. "I'll have to do it."

"Good man."

Another ten minutes passed with Bluebonnet showing even more distress.

Cursing under his breath, Holt began to pace the stall.

"A man with horses in his blood is a cursed man, Colt. It's hell when you have them and hell when you don't. You—"

Colt held up a hand to stop Holt in midsentence. "I see a red bag coming," he said firmly. "Better give me the scalpel."

For the next couple of minutes, Colt blocked everything from his mind, except saving the mare and foal. With a steady hand he sliced through the thick membrane that had protected and nourished the baby for eleven long months but had now become its worst enemy.

Birth water instantly poured from the incision, and thankfully, right behind the flood the baby's front feet emerged. First one hoof, then the other appeared, along with the muzzle.

"Maybe we should pull—to help her," Holt suggested. "Bluebonnet is getting weak."

Colt glanced at the mare. She was exhausted, but he figured the will to have her baby would keep her fighting.

"It's coming easy now, Holt. I think she'll manage."

Colt barely had time to finish speaking before the remainder of the foal slipped out. A huge breath of relief whooshed out of the mare, and Holt made a triumphant fist pump.

"It's a filly," Colt announced. "She appears to be perfect, too."

Holt let out a good-natured groan. "I might've known. Girls usually cause the most trouble. They're worth it, though."

Trouble? If Colt didn't put the brakes on this growing thing he had for Sophia, he was going to meet up with plenty of it. Right now he felt like he was barreling down a steep hill and didn't have any idea what waited for him at the bottom of the draw.

While the uneasy thoughts ran through Colt's mind, he carefully observed the foal. "Well, this little girl looks to be breathing just fine. And she's bigger than I thought she'd be."

Holt drew in a deep breath and after removing his gloves, wiped a hand over his face. "I'm relieved. Now if they're both strong enough to stand and the filly is able to nurse, I'll call Isabelle and give her a happy report." He looked over at Colt. "No need for you to stick around. It might be another hour or so before the baby takes milk. Go on home and get some rest."

Leaving his squatted position over the mare and baby, Colt walked over and picked up a towel Farley had fetched with the medical supplies. "I'm staying," he said, as he wiped his hands. "I feel kind of responsible for them now."

With an understanding nod, Holt patted his shoulder. "I'm grateful."

By the end of the next day, Maureen had made a point to stop by the kitchen and relate the incident of Colt jumping in to help Holt save the mare and filly. Maureen's visit was later followed by Jazelle, who'd told Sophia the whole Hollister family had been singing Colt's praises. Especially Chandler, who'd said the procedure Colt had performed was not for the faint of heart.

Sophia hadn't been surprised to hear about Colt's steady nerves in a stressful situation. True, the only time she'd seen him actually at work, he'd been riding a horse and not facing a life-and-death situation. Still, she'd learned enough about his character to know he wasn't the sort to run from a challenge.

But what about running from a woman, Sophia? Why don't you ask him outright how he feels about settling down with a wife? Or having children of his own? Are you afraid you might find out that he's not interested in having a family?

For the past four days, since learning of the foaling incident, the mocking voice had been rolling over and over in Sophia's mind. But she'd tried her best to ignore the questions. After all, she didn't need to be thinking that far into the future, or wondering if Colt's intentions toward her were serious. It was up to her to decide whether or not she wanted to allow herself to get serious with him.

These past few days she'd only heard from him twice. Once to explain he'd been working overtime and hadn't had a chance to stop by the kitchen to see her. The other message was a reminder about the Christmas party at the Bar X Saturday night and that he'd pick her up at the ranch house at a quarter to seven.

Now, with Saturday evening finally arriving, and forty-five minutes left for her to ready herself for the party, Sophia had to admit she'd been missing Colt.

She was standing in the small bathroom located off the kitchen, dabbing a peach-colored blush onto her cheeks when Jazelle knocked on the partially open door.

"Jazelle! I thought you'd left a long time ago. Aren't you going to the party?"

The housekeeper was carrying her toddler daughter, Madison, on one hip. The baby was clutching a yellow plastic hammer and screeching happily as she tried to bang the toy against her mother's head.

"I am going to the party," she said with a weary but happy smile. "I stayed behind to help Kat get her twins bathed and ready to go. I don't have to tell you that Abby and Andy are a handful. Kat insisted she could handle the pair, but I know she's not feeling well so I offered to give her a hand."

"That was extra nice of you." Sophia looked at her and smiled. "Especially when you have your own little ones to deal with. And Madison looks like she has enough energy to go all night."

Jazelle laughed. "That's when her daddy will be home from his work shift and he'll take over chasing after his daughter, and I'll get a rest. Actually, we're all going to get a rest. Tessa has hired a couple of women to care for the kids while we all enjoy the party."

"Oh. That was a very thoughtful thing for her to do," Sophia commented, then leveled a look of concern at Jazelle. "I hope Kat is feeling well enough to enjoy the Christmas festivities. It would be awful for her to come down with the flu or something right here at the holidays."

Reeva had decided she'd rather spend the evening resting with a book than attending a party with more than a hundred guests and loud music, so she'd left for home nearly an hour ago. Presently, there was no one in the kitchen area except Sophia and Jazelle, but to make sure their conversation remained private, the other woman stepped partially into the bathroom.

"Don't say anything to anyone yet," she said, "but Kat insinuated that she's thinking she might be pregnant."

Sophia was more than surprised. "Kat? Pregnant? I never imagined her... I'm not meaning that she's old, she's probably not more than thirty-five. But she and Blake already have three children, and they both have very busy jobs."

Jazelle's smile was knowing. "Love hardly considers those factors. And Blake and Kat are as much in love now as they were on their wedding day. Anyway, she's up there now doing a home pregnancy test. So I wouldn't be surprised if we hear an announcement tonight at the party."

"If we do, I'll act shocked," Sophia assured her.

Jazelle laughed, then gave her a quick study. "You're looking fabulous tonight. Colt won't be able to keep his eyes off you."

Sophia glanced down at the sparkly cream dress she'd chosen to wear. She'd purchased it for a staff party being given for her boss at West Coast Designs. But she'd ended up turning in her resignation long before the party, and the dress had gone unworn until now.

"Thanks. But I wasn't sure about this dress. I have a red one that I thought might be more appropriate, then I nixed the idea. Being a Christmas party, there will probably be a wave of red dresses without me wearing one. At least for tonight, Colt won't have to see me wearing a cook's apron or my hair twisted into a bun."

"Hmm. You like him a lot. I can tell."

Blushing, Sophia reached for a tube of mascara. *Your lashes are too long to be real. But I can see that they are real.*

Those words and everything else Colt had said to her in that moment they'd shared in the attic had shivered over her like the soft caress of a hand.

"Yes, I like him—more than I should, probably," Sophia replied.

Jazelle frowned. "Why do you say that? Colt seems like a stand-up guy."

"I believe he is."

"Then you don't have any problem," Jazelle told her while grabbing a hold on Madison's arm to prevent her from hammering her forehead.

Laughing at the baby's antics, Sophia said, "You better get out of here, or you'll be late for the party."

Glancing at her watch she said, "Oh my gosh, you're right! I'll see you at the Bar X."

The housekeeper hurried away, and Sophia finished doing her makeup and hair, but all the while Jazelle's comment continued to plague her thoughts.

Sophia's problem wasn't with Colt. It was with herself. She was being naive to expect all men to want marriage and children. And she was a real fool to think any man wanted to waste his time on a woman who was afraid to make love to him. Especially when he'd done nothing wrong to make her afraid. But try as she might, she couldn't quell the fear that once the passion between them cooled, she'd find herself alone and brokenhearted. And possibly pregnant.

A full-length mirror was attached to the back side of the bathroom door, and as Sophia stood in front of it, critically eyeing her image, she promised herself that tonight at the party she wasn't going to let herself fear anything. Not even getting her heart broken.

Colt was amazed that he'd managed to keep the truck from running off the road as he drove Sophia and himself to the Bar X. Eighty percent of the trip, he'd been staring at her rather than the dirt path ahead.

He'd expected her to be dressed up for the festive event, but he'd not planned on her looking like a walking vision. Everything about her dress showcased the full curves of her breasts and the outline of her narrow waist, while the V of the neckline was just deep enough to reveal a bit of smooth cleavage. The top half of her black hair was pulled into a fall of waves and anchored in the center of her crown with a pair of red, glittery barrettes. The color matched her Christmas-red lips, and he couldn't help thinking how he'd like to kiss away her lipstick, then take down her hair and lay her head upon the pillows on his bed.

Oh hell, with this kind of thinking it was going to be a long, frustrating night, he thought.

"You look very handsome tonight, Colt. I like your vest."

The wool-type vest was a dove-gray color and buttoned down the front with a row of small metal buttons. He'd worn it over a western shirt done in black-and-gray paisley. He was a man that didn't make much of a fuss with his appearance, but for tonight, he'd tried. Now her compliment made him glad he'd made an extra effort to look presentable for her.

"Thanks," he said with a grin. "I even pulled out my dancing boots for this party."

She glanced down at the black square-toed cowboy boots on his feet. They were made of quilled ostrich leather and appeared nothing like the old roughout boots he wore while on the job.

"Very nice. Do the soles have holes in them?" she casually asked.

"Holes?" He shot a comical frown in her direction. "Do they look that old?"

She laughed. "No. But I thought they might've had holes from all the dancing you've done with the ladies back in New Mexico."

He slanted her a sly look. "Oh, I see. That was a trick question. Well, when we get out of this truck, I'll lift my foot and show you these are hardly worn."

Another laugh escaped her. "You must have a third pair at home."

His lips took on a clever twist. "Does that make you jealous? To think of me dancing with the ladies?"

"Maybe. A little."

"It shouldn't," he told her. "I never think of anyone back there. Except my dad."

"Honestly?"

"Honestly."

He reached over and clasped her hand in his, and the contact caused Sophia's heart to thump hard in her chest. All this week, she'd thought of little else but seeing him again, feeling the warmth of his touch. Never in the whole time she'd been engaged to Tristen had she felt this obsessed or this full of longing. What did it mean? That she'd never actually loved him at all? That what she was experiencing for Colt was real and true?

Oh Lord, the contradicting thoughts and feelings going on inside of her were confusing. The only thing she was certain about was that she was tired of running from her doubts and fears.

When they arrived at the Bar X, the area around the barn where the party was being held was packed tight with cars and pickup trucks. Colt drove on past the barn for a short distance and parked alongside a dim dirt path.

"This is the way to my house," he told her, pointing in the direction of a high, towering bluff of rock. "It's behind the bluff on the foot of a hill."

As she stood on the ground beside him, her gaze followed the line of his finger. "This is beautiful, Colt. No wonder you have no desire to live elsewhere."

"Wait until you see the view from my house. It's incredible. Like right out of a western painting."

Wait until you see. Apparently he intended for her to visit his home at some point. Tonight? The idea caused everything inside her to buzz with anticipation. If he kissed her again, the way he'd kissed her that night in her grandmother's kitchen, she'd end up being putty in his hands.

"Lucky you," she murmured.

"Yes, lucky me," he said with a grin, then resting a hand against her back, he helped her over the rough ground until they reached the barn of partygoers.

Since the night air was already growing cool, the

big double doors at the end of the barn were closed, and the guests were entering the building through a smaller side door. As Colt and Sophia stepped inside they were greeted by Joseph and Tessa Hollister, the hosts of tonight's celebration.

"Glad you could make the party, Colt. I'm sure the long distance you had to travel to get here must've been a pain," Joseph said jokingly as they shook hands.

Colt chuckled. "Yeah, I was thinking I should ask you to reimburse my fuel cost. Don't worry, I'll take it up in food and drink tonight."

Tessa laughed. "We have plenty of that to go around," she told him, before she stepped forward and gave Sophia a warm hug. "It's good to see you again, Sophia. And wow! You look just like that Italian actress from years ago. What's her name…" She thought for moment, then groaned. "Oh, I can't remember. Anyway, you look incredible."

"You're too kind, Tessa. And how on earth did you manage to get all this done with everything else you have to do?"

Sophia made a sweeping gesture at the interior of the barn. Normally the building was used to store tons of alfalfa hay. For tonight's party, it had been transformed into a Christmas fairyland. High above their heads, rafters were strung with evergreen boughs, thousands of clear, twinkling lights, and red and gold bows sporting long streamers. A few feet from where the two couples stood, a huge pinyon pine was adorned with ornaments of all shapes and sizes. The whole tree was ablaze with colorful blinking lights, including a bright gold star at the very top. Beneath the decorated branches, small packages wrapped in red, blue and green foil were piled high. Beyond the tree, three long tables were heaped with refreshments, some of which were already being sampled by the guests.

"She's like Mom. She's a real wonder," Joseph answered Sophia's question, while giving his wife a loving wink. "She does all this while taking care of our three kids and me, and helping Sam manage the ranch. She makes me feel like a slacker around here."

Since Joseph put in an absurd number of hours on duty as a Yavapai County deputy sheriff, everyone knew he worked as hard or harder than anyone present at the party tonight.

"Don't tell Joe," Tessa teased behind the back of her hand, "but I'm thinking about getting rid of him and finding a man who'll do some real work around here."

They were all laughing at Tessa's remark when Luke and Prudence walked through the door. As the two brothers greeted each other with a partial hug, Sophia extended her hand to Prudence.

Since she'd moved to Three Rivers, the opportunities to talk with Colt's sister-in-law had been limited for Sophia, but the times that they had spoken, the woman had been exceptionally cordial. To be honest, Sophia felt a bit less than average in her presence, and the feeling had nothing to do with the woman being attractive and intelligent. Prudence came from a whole and loving family. One that Luke was no doubt proud to call his in-laws. Whereas Sophia's splintered family was nothing to brag about to Colt.

"I've been hearing about all the delicious things you've been cooking over at the ranch house," Prudence told her. "I'd love for you to give me a few lessons. Luke says my cooking tastes like burnt cardboard. I confess he's much better at it than I am."

"Oh, I doubt that," Sophia said politely.

Luke looked at his wife and chuckled. "She hasn't tasted your biscuits."

"Well, they're good when I take them out of the can and bake them," she said in her defense.

More laughs erupted from the group before Colt wrapped his arm around Sophia's shoulders.

"You guys will have to excuse us," he said to the group. "This talk of food is making me hungry."

Colt walked with her through the growing crowd, and along the way they were greeted by several cowhands who worked for Three Rivers, including Taggart O'Brien and his wife, Emily-Ann.

"In a roundabout way, Tag is the reason Luke and I both moved to Three Rivers," Colt said as they reached the refreshment area.

Sophia picked up a plate from a stack located at

the end of the table. "Oh, I didn't realize that. What's the connection between him and you two brothers?" Sophia asked.

"Tag and Luke have been friends for years. Ever since we all lived in Texas. Tag was hired when Matthew, the prior foreman at Three Rivers, married Camille and took over the management of Red Bluff. And then when Holt decided to give in and hire an assistant, Tag suggested Luke for the position, and as they say—"

"The rest is history," she finished, then glanced thoughtfully over her shoulder to where Taggart and his wife were speaking to Sam, the foreman of the Bar X, who also happened to be Holt's father-in-law. "I'll have to remember to give Tag a big thanks."

"For what?" Colt asked as he forked a tiny crab sandwich onto his plate. "He didn't put in a word for you to be hired as cook, did he?"

She chuckled. "No. Gran did that for me. I was just thinking that if not for Tag, I would've probably gone through life without ever meeting you. And that's an awful thought."

"I agree," he replied. "Never meeting you is an awful thought."

Smiling at him, she said, "You know, the Hollisters consider you a hero for saving Bluebonnet and her foal."

He let out a wry laugh. "If I'm a hero, then you're

Cinderella," he said, then laughed again. "Wait a minute, you are Cinderella, aren't you?"

"Far from it."

He pretended to wipe sweat from his brow with the sleeve of his shirt. "Whew! That's good news. For a few seconds I thought I was going to have to get you home before midnight."

"I'll try not to turn into a cinder girl before then."

While Colt and Sophia enjoyed the food, a live band finished setting up on a small platform at the back of the building and began to play a variety of Christmas tunes. The music definitely livened up the mood of the party, and soon the empty floor was jammed with dancing couples.

When Colt noticed Sophia enthusiastically tapping her toe to the music, he reached for her hand. "Ready to take a whirl with the rest of them?"

"It's been a long while since I've danced, but if you feel like risking toe damage, then I'm ready."

Laughing, he whirled her into his arms and then smoothly guided them into a simple two-step. "Why didn't you warn me beforehand? I would've worn my steel-toed boots."

She squeezed his hand, and Colt was thrilled at how relaxed she felt in his arms, and as they moved gently with the music, he wondered why dancing had never felt like this before. His boots were gliding over the planked wood floor as if they weren't even touching the ground, while the dancers around them had melted into little more than a blur.

"If I had warned you that my dancing skills were rusty, you might've invited some other girl," she said coyly.

His chuckle was low and lusty. "Not a chance."

She smiled up at him, and Colt noticed how the lights above their heads twinkled down on her face and hair. The glow made her look as if she'd been dusted with gold.

"This is what Christmas should be, Colt. Food and music and laughter and celebrating with our friends."

He pulled her a fraction closer. "Glad you came?"

"Very glad. I had forgotten what it was like to go out and be festive like this. It's been a long time."

From the bits she'd revealed about her past, he'd concluded that once her engagement had ended and she'd lost the baby, she must have put parts of her life on hold. Which, in his opinion, had been a terrible mistake. Her ex wasn't worth giving up anything for. But then, he had to remember, she hadn't necessarily been grieving over the breakup with him. She'd been in pain over losing her baby. And that kind of grief was something Colt had never dealt with. He didn't know how to help her move forward. But somehow he had to try.

"I didn't exactly step right off the dance floor when I moved here," he admitted. "To tell you the truth, I'd kind of—well, quit going out to parties or on dates."

Her eyes were wide as she studied his face. "Why? Did you break up with someone special?"

His lips took on a bitter twist. "I haven't had anyone special. At least, not since my college days years ago. There was a time in my freshman year that I wanted to get married. Or I thought I did," he added.

"Married? I'm stunned."

"Yeah. So was my father. Especially after he met the girl and pegged her as plastic. I should've listened to him. But I was hardheaded."

"Imagine that," she said shrewdly. "So what happened?"

"I was practically on my way to the jeweler's to buy an engagement ring when she left me for greener pastures," he told her. "After that I pretty much swore off love and marriage."

"And now? Why had you quit dating?"

"In one word, boredom. I grew tired of the whole meaningless game."

She was silent for long moments, and then her gaze lifted to his. "Do you think the two of us are meaningless?"

Did he? For the past couple of weeks since he'd met her, he'd been asking himself what his intentions toward Sophia could actually be. Three weeks ago, he'd had no desire to even consider the notion that one day he'd be a husband or father. Now, as he looked down at Sophia's lovely face, he knew his thoughts and feelings had made a sudden and total turnaround.

"If I thought we were meaningless, I wouldn't be here…getting my toes squashed."

Laughing softly, she pinched the side of his waist. "Just for that I might really step on them."

"I'm not a bit worried," he said, and as the band began another number, he purposely kept her on the dance floor and in his arms.

Chapter Ten

For the next hour and a half Colt and Sophia spent the time dancing and chatting with friends. And throughout the evening she'd felt the wall she'd erected around her heart melting like sugar in her grandmother's saucepan. But it wasn't until Maureen requested the band to play "The Christmas Waltz," and Colt whirled her around the dance floor, that she felt as though the two of them had entered a fairy-tale world. One that she never wanted to end.

When the timeless song concluded and they walked off the floor, she continued to maintain a tight hold on his arm.

"Would you like more punch, or coffee?" he asked.

Glancing around, Sophia noticed they'd ended up in a far corner of the barn and on the opposite side from the refreshment tables. Behind them was a small exit door, similar to the one where they'd entered the building when they'd first arrived.

Sophia gestured to the door which was only a few steps away. "I was thinking more about going outside and catching a breath of fresh air. Do you think that door might open?"

"Let's go see."

Her arm still wrapped around his, they moved over to the door, which was partially hidden from the crowd by a large support beam. Sophia was waiting for Colt to try the latch when she suddenly spotted the clump of mistletoe hanging over the door and just above his head.

The situation was too tempting for Sophia to pass up. Without a word to reveal her intentions, she tugged him around and promptly proceeded to kiss him squarely on the lips.

"Mmm. Sophia—uh—what—"

Before he could stammer out the last of his question, she pointed impishly up at the green sprig.

"I caught you under the mistletoe," she whispered, then curling her arms around his neck, she touched her lips to his once again. "And now that I have you here, I need to take advantage."

Behind them, she heard the band break into another song and the shuffle of feet as people resumed dancing, but that was all she noticed before she placed a slow and deliberate kiss upon his mouth.

As soon as she eased her head back, she could see the surprise in his eyes. She could also see something else. Like smoke from a simmering fire.

"Do you still want to go outside?" he asked huskily.

"I do."

They stepped into the chilly night, and after Colt shut the door behind them, he didn't hesitate to pull her into his arms.

With his hands cradling her face, he tilted it up toward his. "Sophia, if you're trying to tell me something with that kiss, I'm ready to listen."

Her heart was hammering in her ears as she slid her arms around his waist and pulled herself tight against him. "I want you, Colt. All this past week, you're all I've been able to think about, dream about. Tonight I've realized I don't want to run from this thing between us."

"Sophia."

Her name came out with a rushed breath, and then his lips were on hers, sweeping her away to that magical place, where only he could take her.

She didn't know how long they kissed. The only thing she was vaguely aware of was the nearby bawl of a cow and, directly behind them, the muffled sound of music coming from within the barn. Even the cold air penetrating the thin fabric of her dress didn't faze her.

All she knew was that nothing else mattered but the sweet and glorious feeling of being back in his arms and having his lips devouring hers.

When he finally lifted his head, she opened her eyes to see his face hovering a breath away from hers. And in that moment, she recognized how much she'd grown to want and need him.

"Do you think we, uh, might slip away?" she asked. "Without anyone noticing?"

"Oh, there'll be a few who will eventually notice we're gone," he said. "But I don't care. Do you?"

"No. They can party on without us."

He didn't say anything, but even in the faint moonlight, she could see something flare in his eyes. The look said he wanted her, and that was enough for Sophia.

It took less than three minutes for them to drive to Colt's house. If her senses hadn't been so consumed with the thought of making love to Colt, she would have noticed more about his place. As it was, she scarcely took in that it was built of logs and had a row of steps leading up to a high porch with a railing around it.

Once inside he switched on a lamp, and Sophia barely had time to get a glimpse of a small fireplace and a dark red couch before he was taking her into his arms and fastening his lips to hers.

He kissed her until she was certain there wasn't

an ounce of oxygen left in her lungs and her legs had turned into two sticks of soft rubber.

When he finally eased his mouth away from hers, he nuzzled his nose against the side of her hair. "Do you have any idea how much I want you?"

"It couldn't be as much as I want you," she answered.

Groaning, his lips returned to hers, and after another long, searching kiss, he reached for her hand and silently led her out of the room and down a short hallway.

When they stepped into his bedroom, he avoided turning on the light, but there was enough moonlight streaming through the windows for her to see the dim outline of a queen-size bed with rumpled covers. Other than a few jeans and shirts tossed over the footboard of the bed, the room was tidy. The faint scent of masculine cologne lingered in the air, along with the silence. It reminded her that they were totally and completely alone.

The pressure of his hand on hers increased, and she looked up to see he was studying her face.

"Are you okay with this?" he asked.

"Yes. Why do you ask?"

"Because you look a little…shaky."

"I am shaky. Kissing you makes me that way."

She was expecting him to laugh. Instead, he pulled her into his arms and stroked fingertips along her cheek. "Sophia, I've imagined this moment so often. And now that I have you here—almost in my bed—I can't help but think I don't deserve you."

She was completely caught off guard by the serious tone in his voice and the solemn look on his face. "There's no reason for you to think such a thing."

"I don't know how a cowboy like me ended up with a lady like you."

"Did you ever think that every lady just might really need a cowboy of her own?" she whispered. "And you're mine?"

"I want to believe that," he murmured. "I want to believe everything about tonight."

"Let me show you how real it is," she murmured as she reached for the buttons on his vest.

He allowed her the time to finish unbuttoning the garment and push it off his shoulders, before he reached for the zipper at the back of her dress. As it slid downward, the fabric fell open to expose her bare skin. He paused long enough to flatten his hand against the small of her back and gently rub.

His calloused palm created a delicious friction against her flesh, and like throwing tinder onto an already burning fire, heat flashed up to the roots of her hair and all the way down to the soles of her feet.

"Mmm. You feel like a piece of satin that's been warmed by the fire," he said as he bent his head and placed a row of kisses on the ridge of her shoulder.

Groaning with pleasure, Sophia gripped the waistband of his jeans and fought to keep her knees from buckling. When her head lolled to one side, exposing the creamy line of her throat to his lips, he took advantage of the position and nibbled his way up to her ear. At the same time his fingers pulled the barrettes from her hair and it tumbled down, just like her resistance had crumbled the very first time she'd laid eyes on him.

"And you smell good, too," he told her. "Like a Christmas cookie with lots of vanilla."

She smiled dreamily as he peppered tiny kisses across her cheeks and over the bridge of her nose.

"That's because I'm a cook."

"Then you'd better start bottling the scent," he mouthed against her skin. "I'll buy the first one."

"You're crazy."

"Yes. About you. About this." He touched a forefinger to her lips, then followed it with a tiny kiss. "And having you here with me. In my arms."

His breath was warm on her cheeks, and his lips were ever so tempting as they pressed against her chin and nose and the corners of her mouth.

With her eyes closed and her hands gripping his waist, she let her thoughts go to nothing but him and the incredible sensations that were showering over her.

But as the fire inside her roared higher, her body began to beg for more, and she didn't hesitate to unsnap the pearl buttons on his shirt.

Once the garment had parted, she eagerly raced

her hands over his heated skin, while each finger relished the hard, corded muscles of his abdomen and each separate ridge of his ribs. By the time her palms finally pushed their way up to his nipples, he was growling deep in his throat and gently sinking his teeth into the curve of her neck.

Gasping with need, Sophia pulled away from him and quickly stepped out of her loosened dress. As soon as it fell to the floor, he removed her scanty lingerie and tossed it aside.

His gaze fell on her naked silhouette, and although she'd expected to want to dive beneath the tousled covers on the bed and hide, amazingly she relished the hungry look in his eyes, the faint appreciative smile on his lips.

"I thought you looked incredible in your dress," he said lowly. "But that image can't compare to how you look now."

All the while he was speaking in a husky voice, his head was drawing downward until his lips were hovering over the brown peak of one breast. When it finally closed over the budded nipple, she couldn't help but cry his name and thrust her fingers into his thick, black hair.

The more he nibbled and tugged at the sensitive flesh, the urgency to have their bodies connected was so great her breathing turned into broken pants and her hips thrust ahead to press against the hard erection inside his jeans.

It was a relief when he finally tore his mouth from her breast and quickly began to shed his clothing. Once he was stripped down to a pair of navy briefs, he picked her up and placed her in the middle of the bed, then quickly stretched his long body next to hers.

Sophia immediately rolled toward him and curled her arm tightly around his waist. With her nose pressed to his, she said, "I never thought I'd find the courage to do this—with you."

"But you did. And what are you thinking now?"

"That I wouldn't want to be anywhere else."

"Sophia," he whispered against her cheek, "this is the way it should be with us. The way it's going to be from now on."

From now on. No. Sophia couldn't let that sort of thought creep into her head. She wasn't going to think about tomorrow. It was all about tonight and finding joy in his arms.

The kiss he planted on her lips only served to intensify the aching need to feel him inside her. When her hand slipped inside his briefs and touched his manhood, he sucked in a sharp breath and grabbed her wrist.

"Oh, honey, I don't think… I can hold up to that much from you."

Smiling wickedly, she returned her hand to his waist, then slowly walked her fingers up his arm until they reached his shoulder. These past few minutes his skin had seemed to grow even hotter, and she slipped her hand over him and drew his heat into her, until everything inside her was simmering and waiting to burst into sizzling bubbles.

He nuzzled his nose in the tumbled waves of her black hair. "Are you using some sort of birth control?"

She understood the question had to be asked. It was a very important one. Not only for him but for her, also. Even so, hearing it was like cold water being tossed in her face.

"Yes. I'm on the pill, but I…"

Easing his head back, he said, "What? Don't trust it? Or me?"

"I don't know. It's not something I've had to think about. Not until—" She'd met him and her plan to stay out of a man's bed had crumbled, she thought.

When she didn't go on, he gently stroked her hair from her forehead, before touching his lips to one temple.

"Don't worry, sweetheart," he said gently. "I'll use extra protection. It will be okay."

"Yes. Everything will be okay." It had to be, she thought. Because she couldn't get up and run now. Her heart wouldn't let her.

He eased off the bed and opened a drawer on the nightstand. When he turned his back to her, she realized he was fitting himself with a condom. A part of her was relieved he was taking extra precautions to make sure she wouldn't get pregnant. Yet, there was a piece of her heart that longed to hear him say that if by some chance she got pregnant, he wouldn't desert her. He wouldn't blame her or turn away. But that was a silly, emotional wish. One that she needed to get out of her head.

And thankfully, when he returned to the bed and folded her in his arms, all those torn thoughts vanished. Now, this very moment was all she could think about, and when his lips lowered to hers, she gave herself up to the passion in his kiss.

When Colt finally eased Sophia onto her back and slowly connected their bodies, he was blindsided by the sensations rushing at him. Like a tidal wave, it caught his breath and scattered his senses like pebbles on a stretch of sand.

How could she feel this warm and soft? How could her body fit so perfectly to his? The stunning realization that they'd been especially made for each other darted through his mind. Followed by the regret that it had taken him so long to finally find her.

Somewhere among those spinning thoughts, he had the presence of mind to look down at her. His heart swelled as he noted how the moonlight glowed upon her features and turned her black hair into a silver waterfall of waves against her cheek. Her eyes were closed, yet the smile tilting her lips told him what he needed to know.

"Sophia! This…you… It's all I want."

Her lashes fluttered open, and as her brown eyes met his, something in the middle of his chest broke apart, followed by the flow of a sweet, warm sensation.

"Love me, Colt. Just love me."

Her whispered plea was all he needed to put his body in motion, and she met his thrust with a needy groan. Immediately their arching hips settled into a steady pace.

Colt closed his eyes as he became lost in the pleasure of touching her, feeling her body surrounding him, loving him. He wanted every part of her, and with that realization came the fact that this night would never be enough to quench his desire for her. He was going to need more nights, more time. He was going to need a lifetime.

Recognizing that reality should've acted like a bucket of ice on the fire raging inside of him. Instead, he accepted it like a dying man who'd finally found peace from his demons. All of a sudden she was transforming him into a different man and the hell of it, he didn't care.

As the incredible thoughts raced through his brain, the fire in his loins burned even hotter. Her lips were sliding over his chest, pressing kisses to his breastbone, and then her tongue began to make tantalizing circles around each nipple. At the same time her hands were skimming over his arms and shoulders, then down his back to anchor a hold on his buttocks.

"You taste so good, Colt. Too good."

Her voice was so thick with desire he could barely decipher the words, and the erotic sound was like accelerant to his already raging fire.

He wanted to reply, to tell her exactly what she was doing to him. But he was already climbing to paradise, making it impossible for him to utter anything except a hungry groan.

His thrusts quickened, and she gladly matched the pace he was setting. For long moments he gloried in the road they were taking together, but the pleasure was so intense he could no longer hold back. And neither could she.

Eventually, he felt her body tightening around his. Felt her fingers clenching into his flesh, and then suddenly he heard her broken cry of release. The knowledge that she'd reached the pinnacle of their journey caused his self-control to splinter into a thousand pieces. And then he knew nothing as he floated off to a euphoric place where there was only the two of them bound together, drifting through a soft mist.

Some moments later, Colt managed to open his eyes and discovered his body was still draped over Sophia's. Sweat was streaming into his eyes, while his lungs continued their laboring gasp to regain lost oxygen.

With great effort, he made himself roll his weight

off her, and as he pillowed his head next to hers, she opened her eyes, and the look she gave him was a mixture of dreamy pleasure and dazed confusion. Apparently she was just as stunned as he was by what had just occurred between them.

Reaching over, he slid his hand down her arm and as he took in her tumbled hair and swollen lips, he realized that no matter what words he chose to speak, they were going to sound trite.

"I don't know what to say, Sophia. Except that I'm still shaking."

Closing her eyes, she let out a long breath. "I'm shaking, too. I wasn't expecting this to be so...intense."

Was that the word for it? *Explosive*, *tender*, and *all-consuming*. It had been all those things to Colt and so much more.

He slipped his fingers into her hair. "I didn't hurt you, did I?"

"No. Not at all. It was all incredible—wonderful, in fact." She opened her eyes and looked at him. "I... never knew it could be like that. And I...feel a little stupid."

Not knowing what she could possibly mean, he studied her face. "Is that why you look like you're about to cry?"

Afraid he might be right about her bursting into tears, Sophia rolled away from him and sat up on the side of the bed.

With her back to him, she wrapped a blanket around her to cover her nakedness. "I'm not going to cry," she said firmly.

But in her mind, tears were already beginning to drip and form a dark pool at the bottom of her heart. She'd told Colt she felt stupid, but actually it was far worse than that. She was overwhelmed with icy fear.

"I'm glad," he said. "This is a special time for us. A beginning. And I want you to smile."

Pain ripped through her chest, but she told herself it was best to suffer now, rather than deal with an even worse heartache later.

Bending her head, she pressed both palms to her hot cheeks. "I'm sorry, Colt. But this can't be a... beginning."

She was met with silence, and then he scrambled off the bed. After he'd pulled on his underwear, he sat down next to her, and as his bare leg pressed into hers, Sophia wondered if sometime during their lovemaking, she'd lost all common sense. Any sane woman wouldn't be making passionate love to a man one minute, then in the next telling him it had to end.

"What are you talking about? Didn't we just make love? Didn't you just tell me it was wonderful?"

She fought to swallow away the lump of hot tears in her throat. "Yes, we did. And yes, it was perfect. But I see that sleeping with you was a mistake. Well, at least it was for me. Now it's going to be hard for us to go back to going on casual dates and being friends."

"Damn it, Sophia, why would I want to go back to casual dates? Furthermore, why would you? I don't want to be just your boyfriend! And I think you want more than that from me."

She heard the anger and frustration building in his voice, and though she wasn't surprised by it, the condemning tone made her feel a heck of a lot worse than she already did.

"Sophia, I want us to be together in all the ways a man and woman can be together."

"And what if I got pregnant, Colt? What then?"

His head moved from side to side. "I don't think you're understanding what I'm trying to say. I have no intentions of leaving you for any reason. I want us to be together for a lifetime."

Her breath caught, and all she could do was stare at him in dazed wonder.

"Are you hinting at marriage?" she asked in a hoarse voice.

He cursed under his breath. "I'm not hinting at it, I'm telling you straight-out. I love you. I want to be your husband. I want you to be my wife."

There was no way he could imagine how much she wanted to believe him. To think of them building a life together as a married couple was like a fairy tale. Something she could only hope for in her wildest dreams.

"Listen, Colt, only three weeks ago, you told me you hadn't dated for months. That tells me you weren't the least bit interested in marriage or having children."

"It's true that I had stopped seeing women. And maybe I wasn't interested in marriage or having children. But that was then. This is now."

Incredulous, she stared at him. "I'm supposed to believe that you've had a sudden change of heart?"

"Why not? Can't a guy change his mind? Or is he supposed to be punished because he's suddenly had his eyes opened?"

"By me? No. I can't believe that. And anyway, I've already had marriage promised to me before. I wore a diamond ring for a few months, and I believed my fiancé actually loved me. But in the end it was all phony. I don't want or need that kind of pretense from you—or any man."

"Don't make the mistake of thinking I'm the same kind of guy you left in California," he said flatly. "Our engagement would be real and true."

"I'm not ready to take that chance."

His fingers tightened ever so slightly on her shoulders, and Sophia had to fight hard to keep from throwing herself back into his arms. But pride and a bucketload of fear gave her the strength to ease away from his hold and reach for her clothing on the floor.

He said, "You're not willing to take the chance because you're afraid, Sophia. Afraid I'm just another bastard out to use you."

He made it sound so awful, she thought, as she

stepped into her panties. Probably because deep in her heart, she knew he was right. But being aware of the problem and being capable of fixing it were two different things. And she couldn't help that her past was still standing like a cold wall of fear to any happiness she might find in her future.

Pulling the straps of her bra onto her shoulders, she looked at him. "I guess I am afraid, Colt. But can you blame me?"

He stood and reached for his jeans. "No. I blame myself for being stupid enough to put my heart on the line again!"

She stepped into her dress and managed to zip it without asking for his help. "I'd be grateful if you'd take me home. I'm…not in the mood for any more Christmas festivities tonight."

He didn't bother to look at her. "Sure. Looks like our party is over, anyway."

Twenty minutes later, Colt felt numb with pain as he braked his truck to a halt in front of Reeva's house and cut the engine.

Sophia's one-eighty had not only left his head whirling, it had also filled him with an anger that was mostly directed at himself. Had he misjudged her so badly? All along he'd thought she was a compassionate woman who'd meant it when she'd kissed him and held him so tightly. Now he could only wonder if she'd ever really cared anything about him.

She sighed, then surprised him completely by reaching across the console and taking hold of his hand.

"I know you're angry with me, Colt. And I'm sorry if I've hurt you. That was never my intention. I don't regret what happened, but after we went to bed together—well, I realized I'm just not ready for this much—this quick. It will be best for me—for the both of us—not to see each other again."

Her words left him chilled to the bone. "You think you know what's best for me?"

"We both know what will happen if we keep seeing each other. I'll wind up in your bed. And I can't deal with that. Not now. I don't know, Colt, maybe I'll never be able to let myself love and trust again. That's why you need to forget me. Forget we were ever together."

He stared at her in disbelief. Forget? Did she expect him to simply wipe her memory from his heart? Was it going to be easy for her to walk away and forget him? No. He couldn't believe that.

"You're lying to me and to yourself, Sophia. You probably can't admit that to yourself right now. But later you're going to wake up and realize what you're throwing away."

Her lips clamped to a thin line. "I'm trying not to hurt you. I'm trying to be sensible."

"No. You're trying to play it safe."

Her gaze dropped guiltily away from his. "Maybe

I am. That should be enough to prove I'm not ready for a relationship."

She was running scared, but he wasn't going to keep hammering home that point to her. Right now she wouldn't let herself imagine the two of them being together, and there was nothing he could do to change her mind.

He let out a heavy sigh. "Okay, Sophia. I'll keep my distance."

Tossing her coat and handbag over her arm, she reached for the door handle. "Don't bother seeing me to the door. I can make it on my own."

"What's wrong? Afraid you might want to kiss me good-night?" he taunted.

"Good night, Colt."

She climbed out of the truck and, without a backward glance, slammed the door shut behind her.

Colt started the engine, but he didn't pull away until she was safely inside the house and the porch light went dark.

It was all incredible. Perfect. Sleeping with you was a mistake. It's best we don't see each other again.

Fragments of her words haunted him as he steered the truck down the dusty road. But it wasn't until he drove past his brother's house that their context drove a stake right into his heart.

He'd been a fool for thinking he could have the same sort of wonderful family that Luke had with

Prudence. Now, instead of this Christmas being the best he'd ever had, it was going to be the loneliest time of his life.

Chapter Eleven

It wasn't until the next afternoon, after Sophia and Reeva had fixed a light lunch for the Hollisters and sat down themselves to eat at the kitchen booth, that her grandmother commented on her droopy appearance.

"For you to have gone to one of the biggest parties of the year, you certainly don't act like you enjoyed it," Reeva said as she sipped at a glass of iced tea. "I realize living here is nothing compared to Los Angeles, but I'm sure Tessa and Joe did things up right."

Sophia tried not to sigh. She didn't want to tell Reeva about the break she'd made with Colt. Her grandmother thought Colt hung the moon, and Sophia knew Reeva wouldn't understand why she'd ended things.

How the heck could she understand, Sophia? You don't even understand it yourself. It's like Colt told you. You're a big coward. You don't want to focus on being happy or loving again. You want to hold on to the pain and hurt of the past.

"Sophia, did you hear anything I said?"

Shaking her head against the condemning voice in her ears, Sophia determinedly focused on her grandmother.

"Yes, Gran. I heard you. And I told you Joe and Tessa put on a great party. The barn looked beautiful. And the food was all delicious—even if we didn't cook it," she added in an attempt to lighten the moment.

Reeva frowned at her. "Okay, I'm going to quit beating around the bush. What's happened with you and Colt?"

Sophia suddenly feigned a great interest in the chicken salad on her plate. "What makes you think anything has happened?"

"Because you look like you haven't had a minute's sleep."

That was true, too, Sophia thought, while wondering how her grandmother could read her so well. After Colt had taken her home, she'd immediately undressed and gone to bed. But instead of sleeping, she'd cried for hours. A fact that had made her very angry with herself. Ever since the debacle with Tristen, she'd vowed to never cry over any man.

"Maybe that's because we danced most of the night and I'm tired."

Reeva muttered a curse. "Don't lie to me."

Losing what little grip she had left on her emotions, Sophia slapped her fork down on the tabletop. "All right! I've messed up, Gran! I've fooled around and let myself get way too close to Colt. And last night I...well, I told him we needed to stay away from each other."

Instead of cursing a blue streak at her like Sophia had expected, Reeva merely shook her head in disappointment.

"Oh, honey, I thought... I had so much hope for you two. I thought you'd finally put all that mess with Tristen and the baby behind you."

Sophia stared unseeingly at a spot on the opposite end of the kitchen. "How can I put that totally behind me, Gran? It was a hard-learned lesson from a mistake I don't want to repeat. What if I got pregnant? Would Colt want to hang around then?" she asked bluntly.

"I believe Colt is a responsible man. If he loves you, he'd hang around no matter what," she said, then reached across the table and patted the top of Sophia's hand. "You have to start believing in yourself and trusting him. Otherwise, you're going to wind up living a cold, lonely life."

Sighing, Sophia looked regretfully at her grandmother. "All right. Colt did say he loved me, Gran. He even told me that he wanted to marry me."

Reeva nodded knowingly. "The way I see it, Sophia, you don't have a problem. A good man wants to share his life with you."

Sophia groaned helplessly. "Yes, I agree that Colt is a good man. But I can't forget that Tristen said those same things to me and look what happened. He'd been lying about truly loving me. Lying about wanting a family."

"Not every man is deceitful, Sophia. Surely you don't believe Colt is that sort of man."

Shaking her head, Sophia said, "No. Colt is an honest person. But we've not known each other for very long. Maybe it's too soon for him to know how he really feels about me. I couldn't bear it, Gran, if I let myself believe Colt and then later have him tell me he'd made a mistake about the two of us."

"The misery on your face tells me your heart is already breaking from being apart from Colt."

Yes, her heart was breaking, Sophia thought. Everything inside her felt as though she was on the verge of shattering to pieces.

"I've been wondering if I should leave the ranch and go live in northern California close to Dad. We've been talking quite a bit, and I'm certain he'd welcome me."

"Of course he'd welcome you. And I think it

would be a good thing for you to visit him. Let him see for himself that you've not allowed Liz to warp your opinion of your father. But moving there is the last thing you should do."

"Why?"

Reeva rolled her eyes. "Why? Because this is your home now. I know it, and so do you. More than that, you'd only be running. You can't run from life forever, Sophia. What you need to be thinking is how to make up for this terrible wrong you've done to Colt."

Sophia stared at her with disbelief. "A terrible wrong? For trying to use common sense?"

Reeva's lips pursed with disapproval. "It's terrible when you hurt a person who believes you care deeply about them. You, especially, ought to know that, Sophia. And you've hurt Colt. Don't try to convince me that you haven't."

She'd been trying to tell herself that she'd only hurt Colt's ego and not his feelings. But deep down she feared her grandmother was right and the idea sickened her. She'd never intended or wanted to hurt Colt. She cared about him so much. No, that was wrong, she thought. She loved him so much.

Tears suddenly sprang to her eyes, and she snatched up her napkin and quickly dabbed at the moisture that threatened to fall upon her cheeks.

"Oh, Gran, I'm so stupid. I thought I could keep myself from falling in love with Colt. But last night

I realized I'd failed miserably. I love him. But I don't know what to do about it."

"I'll tell you what you're going to do. You're going to dry your eyes and smile. Everything is going to be all right."

Sophia shot her grandmother a weary smile. "And how could you possibly be so sure that everything will turn out right?"

Reeva winked at her. "Because Christmas is coming, and that's when wishes come true."

"One of the hands took the tire to the tractor shed and tried to repair the flat," Blake told Colt as the two men stared at the empty wheel well on the sleigh. "But the tube was ruined. And so was the tire. We don't have any to fit it, and neither does the tire service in town. But they've ordered one, and it should arrive tomorrow afternoon."

"Well, guess that cancels the sleigh rides for tonight."

Colt was surprised at how disappointed he was over the delay. For the past three days since the Christmas party, he'd not been able to focus on any sort of holiday celebrations. Not with Sophia consuming his thoughts. But Maureen had planned for him to take the kids on their first sleigh ride this evening, and he'd been hoping a rowdy romp through the chaparral and Joshua trees would lift his spirits. Now that plan had been put on hold.

Blake glanced at him. "No need to look so gloomy, Colt. You'll get to drive that team of grays soon enough."

Did he look gloomy? He'd been trying hard to hide his misery. But apparently he needed to try harder.

"I was only thinking about the kids," Colt replied. "They're going to be disappointed."

"Mom hasn't sprung the surprise of the sleigh on them yet. So they can't be disappointed over something they don't know about. Anyway, the kids have plenty to get into without a sleigh ride tonight. Vivian and Sawyer have come down with Hannah and their twin boys. And about an hour ago, Camille and Matthew arrived with little Carter. When the slew of cousins come together, they always have a rip-roaring time."

Blake's mention of his gathering family only deepened Colt's despair. Which didn't make a whole lot of sense. He'd never imagined himself a husband and father. Sophia had been right about that. Having a family of his own hadn't even been a blip on his radar. But then he'd met Sophia, and she had changed him. She'd rearranged every kind of plan he'd ever made for himself.

"Sounds like your whole family will be here for Christmas," Colt said, stating the obvious.

"Yeah, the house is bulging at the seams. But that makes the celebrating even merrier." He chuckled and jerked a thumb behind him where a group of penned mama cows were bawling loudly for their just-weaned babies. "If you see me down here with the cows, you'll know I needed a break from all the noise."

"Right. This is a quiet little spot on the ranch," Colt said in an attempt to joke. "By the way, Blake, I hear Kat is expecting. Congratulations. You must be excited."

Because Colt and Sophia had left the dance early, they'd missed the announcement of Kat's pregnancy. It wasn't until the next morning that Holt had filled him in on the news.

The ranch manager grinned from ear to ear. "Thanks. It's the best Christmas gift ever. Now we're wondering if it will be twins again. After Kat and I had a set and then Vivian had twin boys, we've decided it isn't anything in the water. It's the Hollister genes."

"Two for the price of one. Can't beat that kind of deal," Colt said in the cheeriest voice he could muster.

Laughing, Blake slapped him on the shoulder. "Good thinking. If it turns out that Kat's having twins again, I'll tell her she's saving us money."

Just as Colt forced out a chuckle, Blake's phone dinged with an incoming message. After scanning it quickly, he shook his head.

"I leave my desk for ten minutes and it's like I've

been gone for ten days. Flo needs me at the office," he said wryly. "See you later, Colt."

Colt watched Blake stride off in the direction of the cattle barn, then glanced ruefully at the side-lined sleigh.

He'd been planning on taking Sophia on a sleigh ride with him and the children. But that had been before they'd made love and she'd made the decision to end things between them, he thought miserably.

Walking closer to the sleigh, Colt rested a hand on the front seat and fought to push Sophia's image from his mind. But he wasn't winning the battle. Everywhere he looked, he saw her sweet face smiling up at him. He saw her black hair fanned out on his pillow and her parted lips waiting for his kiss.

If anything, these past days they'd been apart had shown him just how empty his life would be without her. But how was he going to fix things between them? Could he fix them?

He'd considered calling her, but he feared she'd see his name and ignore it. He'd thought about sending her a message, but that didn't feel personal enough. Then there was the most obvious option: stop by the kitchen and see her. But he couldn't bring himself to go near the ranch house. Because he had the sinking feeling she would refuse to talk to him, and where would that leave him? Looking like an idiot and feeling even worse.

Sighing heavily, he left the shed where the sleigh

was parked and headed back to the horse barn. Dusk wasn't far off, and he wanted to make sure the hands had everything tended to before they wound things up for the evening.

Entering the building through the back entrance, he walked past the tack room, then, realizing the door was open and a light was on inside, he stopped and backed up. Riding was finished for the day, and the tack should've already been cleaned and stored away.

Stepping inside, Colt spotted his brother sitting on an overturned keg, adjusting the curb strap on a bridle.

"Luke, what are you doing bothering with that?" Colt asked him. "You should be heading home."

Rising to his feet, Luke hung the bridle on a peg on the wall, then turned back to Colt. "The strap broke. I wanted to get it fixed before tomorrow."

"Tomorrow is Christmas Eve. Holt has given you the day off, and so he should. You've been working like the devil here lately."

Luke slanted him a meaningful glance. "So have you."

"I like it that way."

Hanging his thumbs over the edge of his jeans pockets, Luke rocked back on his heels and continued to study Colt.

"Prudence and I would like you to come over tomorrow before we all gather at the Hollisters. We'll have some cider or something, and then I thought we might FaceTime Dad. He'd enjoy seeing both of us wishing him a merry Christmas."

"Sure, though I'm not sure I want him to see my face."

Stepping closer, Luke peered comically at him. "I don't see anything wrong with your face. Course, it never was as pretty as mine."

Any other time Colt would've laughed at his brother's joke. Instead, he barely managed a grunt. "Looks aren't the problem. Dad has always been able to read me like a book. I don't want him to notice that I'm miserable. He'd get to worrying, and that would ruin his whole Christmas. And I don't want to be responsible for that. Especially now that he's finally invited his neighbor lady to spend the holiday with him."

Luke raised an eyebrow. "Would Dad be right in guessing you're miserable?"

A quick denial was on Colt's tongue, but he rapidly bit it back. What was the use in trying to fool his brother, of all people? If he couldn't be open and honest with Luke, then who could he be frank with?

Heaving out a heavy breath, Colt walked over and rested a hip against a wooden saddle rest. "I don't like admitting it, Luke, but I feel like I'm in the pit of a dry well."

Luke grimaced. "Let me guess. Sophia?"

Colt rubbed a hand across his face. "She says we

shouldn't see each other again. That she's not ready for a relationship. Hell, you know what that means, Luke. It's just a nicer way of saying it's over."

Luke's expression turned dubious. "What brought this on? You two looked awfully tight at the Christmas dance four nights ago."

If they'd been any tighter they would've crushed each other, Colt thought glumly. Now, he couldn't even bring himself to get close enough to get a good look at her.

"Let's just say I was getting too serious for her liking."

Luke's brows pulled together. "Serious? You?"

Colt scuffed the toe of his boot against the worn planks. "Hell, don't look so shocked, Luke. I've already had enough trouble trying to convince Sophia I'm not pretending."

"Okay, if you say you're serious about her, then I believe you." His thoughtful gaze roamed over Colt's face. "Come to think of it, I've never seen you in this sort of state over a woman before. Your feelings for her must be genuine."

Colt let out a groan of frustration. "They are genuine. But she's... Well, she's been hurt, Luke. She doesn't trust me—or herself—or anything about making a future with me." He swiped another hand over his face, then leveled a dejected gaze on his brother. "I probably shouldn't tell you this, but a year or so ago she miscarried a baby. After the father of the child had dumped her. I don't believe she cares about the guy anymore, but the whole ordeal has scarred her."

"That's tough, Colt." Luke shook his head. "She's probably thinking all men are real bastards. And you can't blame her."

"I don't care what opinion she holds of other men. All I want is for her to believe in me—trust *me*." He let out a rough sigh, then folded his arms against his chest. "I'm beginning to wonder if I made a mistake moving out here, Luke. At least if I'd stayed in New Mexico, I wouldn't be in this horrid state of mind."

"No. You'd be listening to women talk about their highlights and manicures. You'd be having some truly meaningful relationships and not have a thing to worry about," Luke said with a heavy dose of sarcasm, then in a serious tone added, "Sorry, Colt. But you're thinking like a fool."

"Yeah. I admit that I am. I love this place. The ranch feels like a real home to me. I wouldn't ever leave."

"What about Sophia? Do you think she's contented living and working here on the ranch?"

Colt frowned thoughtfully. "Yes, I do. Although, she did mention leaving if I didn't stay away from her."

To Colt's amazement Luke let out a huge laugh.

"Brother, you need to quit worrying. Sounds like she's crazy about you."

"Oh, sure, Luke. That's some great reassurance. The woman says she'll run if I even try to get close."

Luke walked over and pretended to punch Colt's jaw with his fist. "Listen, Colt. You need to get a backbone and convince Sophia that you love her. The rest will take care of itself."

"Like that's going to be an easy mission," Colt muttered.

"It will be easy if you just go to her and tell her what's in your heart. And exactly how much you love her." He poked a finger against Colt's chest, then grinned. "See you later. I'm heading home."

Colt thoughtfully watched his brother leave the tack room, then turned out the light. He was bolting the door behind him when Holt approached him from the opposite end of the barn.

"Hey, Colt, I heard about the sleigh tire." He was grinning as he walked up to him. "Bet you're really cut up over that development."

Colt didn't bother to explain that he actually was disappointed. It was all too complicated to try. "I was looking forward to driving the grays," he said. "But Blake says we'll have the tire and be ready to go tomorrow night."

"That's good news for the kids, but I don't know about you." Chuckling, he gave Colt a fond whack on the arm. "When you finish here at the barn, why don't you come by the big house? Isabelle and I are going to stay for a while and visit with my sisters. I don't have a chance to see them all that much. We'll sit around the fireplace and have some drinks."

Since Colt had taken the job with Three Rivers, he'd met both Hollister sisters, Vivian and Camille, and talked with them briefly. Like Maureen, they were both strong and vibrant women. Under different circumstances, he would've enjoyed hearing about Vivian's career as a park ranger and Camille operating her own diner. But in this gloomy mood, he doubted he'd catch half of the conversation.

He said, "Sounds nice, Holt. Thanks for asking. But I'm doing barn watch tonight."

Holt looked surprised. "What about Morgan? Don't tell me he tried to weasel out of the job."

Colt shook his head. "Not at all. He insisted he was happy to stay at the barn tonight, but I sent him home. Doll Brown might go into labor, and if she does I want to be here to see after her."

The bay was one of the older brood mares in Holt's stable, and from the first moment Colt had met her, he'd fallen in love with her soft eyes and the kisses she'd pressed to his cheek.

"That wasn't necessary, Colt. Chandler will be home tonight. If Doll Brown started to deliver, all Morgan would've had to do was pick up the phone and call the house."

Colt shook his head. "No matter, Holt. I'll feel better about being here myself."

"Suit yourself. Would you like me to send someone down with something to eat or drink?"

Someone like Sophia? No. Before he saw her
again, he needed time to think and figure out where
he was going to find the courage to say the words
I love you. And even if he did manage to speak his
feelings aloud, would it make any difference to her?

The next day, Christmas Eve, Sophia and Reeva
had extra help in the kitchen with Maureen, Camille,
Vivian and Jazelle all joining in to get everything
ready for the family party to be held tonight, along
with making a few dishes ahead of time for the big
dinner tomorrow.

By five that evening Maureen declared kitchen
duty completed and insisted that Reeva and Sophia
join in the family celebration. Sophia was hardly in
a festive mood, but she didn't want to appear to be a
party pooper, especially with her grandmother agreeing to fix herself up and join in the fun.

Now that everyone had gathered in the huge den
for drinks and all types of finger foods, Sophia sat
talking with Camille, whose passion was also cooking and managing her diner. Though, as much as
she liked the beautiful redhead, it was still a mental battle for Sophia to remain focused on their conversation.

A few minutes prior, she'd seen Luke, Prudence
and their baby son arrive. She'd expected Colt to

be with them, but so far she'd not seen any sign of him. Which, to some extent, was a relief. After all, what could she say to him? *Sorry, Colt, but you made such perfect love to me that I had to run like a scared chicken? Because I knew something that good couldn't last?*

"Are you expecting someone to show up, Sophia?" Camille asked, as she sipped from a mug of hot cider. "You keep looking around the room."

Trying not to blush, she said, "Uh…no. I was just noticing how the whole Hollister family is here. And everyone is having a good time."

Smiling, Camille nodded. "It is such fun when we're all together like this. And Matthew considers my brothers to be his, too. So he loves it when we come up for a visit."

Camille suddenly yelped with surprise as Hannah, Vivian's teenage daughter, slipped up behind her aunt and placed both hands over her eyes.

"Guess who?"

"Like I wouldn't know it's you, Hannah," Camille said with a laugh. "I can smell horse on you a mile away."

Giggling with delight, the pretty blonde girl smacked a kiss on Camille's cheek, before she walked over and gave Sophia an affectionate hug.

"Sophia, you look gorgeous. I want that skirt and the blouse to go with it," she said, while eyeing Sophia's ankle-length red-and-green-plaid skirt and white blouse. "You look like you're ready for Christmas."

Camille leveled an amused look on her niece. "You're right. Sophia does look stunning. But what would you do in a long skirt like that? You couldn't ride a horse in it."

"Betcha I could," Hannah bragged, then playfully wrinkled her nose at Camille. "But I wouldn't. In a couple of months, Mom and Dad are going to start letting me go on real dates...well, sort of. As long as there's another couple going along, too. But I'll still get to dress up. And I'm old enough to wear a skirt like that. I'm going to be seventeen!"

Sophia smiled at the teenager, who was presently dressed in a denim miniskirt with a bright red sweater with a fuzzy image of Santa's face on the front. "You're dressed up tonight, and you look very pretty."

"Thanks, Sophia. But I'm just me," she said with an exaggerated sigh.

"Yes, and aren't we all lucky that you're just you," Camille said matter-of-factly.

About that time, Hannah spotted Nick, Blake's teenage stepson, approaching them, and she quickly jumped to her feet.

"There's Nick!" she announced as though a prince had just entered the room. She tossed the two women an impish grin. "He's trying to keep the gift he bought me for Christmas a surprise. But I'm going to get him to spill the beans."

Hannah hurried over to the tall, dark-haired young man, and he promptly reached for her hand.

Thoughtfully studying the pair, Camille said, "I wonder how Nick is going to take the idea of Hannah dating? He's about three years or so younger than her. And Kat says he doesn't seem to be that interested in dating—yet."

Sophia said, "Gran tells me that the two cousins have been very close since they were children."

"Hmm. Inseparable is more like it. But when Vivian married Sawyer and moved to his home on the Yavapai Apache Reservation, it put some distance between the two kids. But it hasn't seemed to hurt their bond. And we all have to remember they are cousins only by marriage."

Sophia was thinking about the young couple and how devoted they'd been to each other over the years, when Maureen suddenly entered the doorway of the den. After motioning to the pair of teenagers, she signaled for Sophia to join her.

"Excuse me, Camille, I think your mother needs me."

Rising from her seat at the end of the couch, Sophia made her way across the den to where Maureen was standing in the doorway with Nick and Hannah at her side. The two people had already donned jean jackets and cowboy hats.

"The sleigh is ready for its first riders," Maureen said happily. "Colt has it parked out front, and Vivian and Kat are ready to load their twins, so you three go on."

Colt and the sleigh! Early this morning, Sophia had thought about Maureen's plans to give the children sleigh rides, but she'd been so busy throughout the day that she'd put it out of her head. After her bitter parting with Colt four nights ago, Sophia had already decided she was going to avoid the sleigh, even if she had to hide in a closet. She might have known Maureen would catch her off guard and deliberately throw her at Colt.

"Yippee! This is going to be fun!" Hannah said excitedly.

Nick tugged on her hand. "Come on! Let's go!"

"Make sure you watch out for the twins!" Maureen called out to the two teenagers who were already hurrying down a hallway that would lead them to the front of the house.

Sophia watched them go and wondered what kind of excuse she could come up with to remain in the house. "Maureen, I—"

Seeing the hesitancy on her face, Maureen frowned. "Don't just stand there. Get your coat and go!"

"I don't think… Maybe you should let someone else go in my place. I'm not sure—"

"That you want to sit that close to Colt in the

moonlight?" Not bothering to wait for Sophia's answer, she caught hold of Sophia's arm and marched her down the hallway. "Forget about getting a coat. You can let Colt keep you warm."

Knowing Maureen was just as stubborn as she was beautiful, Sophia didn't try to protest. She simply allowed the woman to lead her through the house and down the porch.

When they finally reached the sleigh, Hannah and Nick were already sitting in the back with the two sets of twins, all of whom were bundled up in coats and sock caps.

Dropping her hold on Sophia, Maureen said, "Hold up, Colt. You have a last-minute passenger."

Colt looked around, and the moment his gaze met hers, Sophia felt her heart make a crazy leap, then settle into a mad gallop. The four days she'd been away from him suddenly felt like an eternity, and her eyes couldn't drink in his image fast enough.

He wrapped the reins around the brake handle, then climbed down to help her into the sleigh. Sophia glanced over her shoulder to see that Maureen had gone over to join Kat and Vivian, who were standing on the bottom step and waiting to wave them off.

"Hello, Sophia," he greeted.

"Hello," she said thickly.

Cupping a hand beneath her elbow, he helped her into the front seat. Once she was settled, he skirted the front of the sleigh to take up his position beside her. Sophia noticed that, unlike her thin blouse, he was wearing his sherpa-lined denim jacket over a red flannel shirt.

Reaching for the reins, he asked, "Are you ready for this?"

If he was talking about the sleigh ride, yes, she was ready. But seeing him again? No. She was a trembling mess. And what could she say to him? That she'd been a fool? That she'd missed him so much these past few days that she was aching from it? Maybe that would be a start to repair the mess she'd made. On the other hand, he might not even care.

"As ready as I'll ever be," she told him.

He wrapped the reins between the fingers of both hands and clucked to the matching mares. The sleigh rolled forward, and the squealing children waved at the women on the steps. Colt urged the horses to pick up their pace, and as they broke into a gentle trot, the bells on their harnesses jingled merrily.

He glanced in her direction. "You didn't wear a coat."

Sophia wasn't about to tell him what Maureen had suggested. That he should keep her warm. "I didn't have time to fetch one."

"There's a blanket under the seat," he told her. "You might want to throw it over you."

That night as she'd sat on the side of his bed, she'd thrown a blanket around her to cover her nakedness from him. Or so she'd told herself that was the reason. In truth, she'd been shaking with fear. And all because she'd come to the realization of how very much she loved him.

Oh God, if she'd been a woman with any kind of strength, she would've confessed her feelings to him right then and there. Instead, she'd hammered a wedge between them.

"If I get too cold, I will."

After passing the ranch yard and the clusters of barns and corrals, Colt guided the horses into a right turn and down a hard-packed road that led between spirals of rock and twisted juniper. About a half mile onward, he made another right turn, and soon they were traveling over a dim trail that wound through a patch of Joshua trees and tall, statuesque saguaros.

The horses responded perfectly to the commands Colt directed to them through the reins in his hands, and as the pair trotted through the desert landscape, Sophia looked up at the night sky and thought about all the lonely Christmases she'd spent in California. Her mother had always been there, but not really there, either. Liz had been too busy entertaining her friends to notice Sophia sitting quietly.

The memories had her glancing over at Colt's strong profile, and she realized that in spite of the wall she'd tried to erect between him and herself, he was still here beside her. He'd told her he would never leave her, and she had to believe him. She had to open her heart and trust him. Otherwise, she had no chance for love or a home and family of her own.

Behind them, the young children were chattering with excitement, kicking their feet and attempting to bounce up and down on the seat, in spite of being fastened in with safety belts.

Glancing over his shoulder, Colt said to Hannah and Nick, "I hope you two are keeping a tight hold on the little ones. I don't think they can wiggle out of those seat belts, but keep an eye on them anyway."

"We will," Nick told him, and then to make sure, he fastened an arm around Johnny's and Jacob's shoulders.

Hannah curved a protective arm around Abagail and Andy. "No problem, Colt. We'll take care of these little monkeys."

"Santa's sleigh! We're riding in Santa's sleigh!" Abby shouted.

"We're going after toys," Andy told his sister. "And they're only for boys. Not for girls."

Johnny and Jacob obviously approved of their cousin's remark. Both little boys giggled and clapped.

When Hannah immediately reprimanded her little cousin for leaving his sister out, Colt cast a faint smile at Sophia.

"Hannah sounds just like her grandmother. And sometimes you sound just like yours."

In spite of her heavy heart, Sophia had to smile at that.

"Gran is partying with the whole family tonight. It's so nice to see."

"Christmas is a time for being together," he said.

A hollow ache settled in her chest, and she swallowed hard as she reached over and rested her hand on his knee.

"I'm learning that, Colt."

He darted an uncertain look at her. "I think we need to talk, Sophia."

"Yes. We do."

She scooted closer to his side, and though they didn't talk any more during the remainder of the ride, hope flickered inside her.

Her grandmother had told her that Christmas was a time for wishes to come true. And her deepest wish was to have Colt's love. She had to believe and trust that miracles really did happen.

Chapter Twelve

When they finished the ride and returned to the front of the house, another group of children were waiting for their turn in the sleigh.

Colt helped Sophia down to the ground and promised he'd find her at the house after he was finished with the sleigh rides. Sophia told him she'd be waiting and went on to join the party that was still going strong.

It wasn't until much later, when Sophia noticed all the children had returned to the house and there was no sign of Colt, that she began to worry. Even if he had changed his mind about talking with her, she seriously doubted he would avoid making an appearance at the party. Not only were his brother and sister-in-law there, but he respected the Hollisters too much to deliberately avoid them on Christmas Eve.

She considered asking Holt or Luke if they knew where Colt was or what he might be doing. But the men appeared to be in deep conversation with Chandler, and she didn't want to interrupt them. Especially when they'd probably think she was overreacting.

But finally, the worry became too much for her. After donning a coat that she'd left hanging in the mudroom, she slipped out a back door of the house and walked rapidly toward the horse barn. If he was still on the ranch, the barn was the only place she could think of that he might be.

Colt finished the last sleigh ride and had settled the gray mares comfortably in a little patch with a loafing shed for shelter from the weather. He was heading back to the house, thinking about everything he was going to say to Sophia, when an odd feeling struck him. Suddenly it was like a hand was against his back pushing him toward the horse barn.

Presently there was no one on watch duty at the barn. Holt had given all the men the night off to allow them a chance to enjoy Christmas Eve. He'd assured Colt that after the gathering with his family ended, he'd come to the barn himself and spend the remainder of the night. But Colt couldn't ignore the hand that seemed to keep propelling him forward.

And moments later, he was grateful he hadn't.

At Doll Brown's stall, he discovered the mare lying on her side, straining with pain. Sweat had soaked her flanks and neck, and there was evidence on the floor of the stall that her water had broken sometime earlier.

Grabbing his cell phone from his pocket, he punched Holt's number. But to his dismay, instead of ringing, there was no sound at all. Desperate, he tapped Chandler's number, but the same thing happened.

Cursing, he looked at the phone and was stunned to see there was no signal. How could this be happening now? No one ever had a problem with phone signals here at the ranch yard.

Deciding he had to get help, he left the stall long enough to race down to Holt's office to use the landline. After fumbling around for the light switch, he rushed over to the desk and jerked up the phone, only to find it was also dead.

In total disbelief, he slammed the receiver back on its hook and trotted back to Doll Brown's stall. The mare was still on her side grunting with pain. She rolled her eyes pleadingly up to Colt as if to say *Don't leave me. Help me.*

His heart heavy with fear, he realized he didn't have time to run all the way to the ranch house to collect Chandler and then make the return trip to the barn. By then, she and the foal might both be gone.

Squatting on his heels, he gently stroked her neck.

"Looks like it's just you and me, girl. We'll do this together. Just hang on."

"Colt! Colt, are you in here?"

Sophia's voice was like a beacon of light in a dark pit, and he straightened to his full height and called out to her.

"Over here, Sophia! Grab that lantern off the support beam. I need your help!"

In a matter of seconds, she was at the stall gate and he opened it to let her inside.

Her worried gaze swung from Colt to the mare and back again. "What's the matter? Is this horse sick?"

"It's Doll Brown. She's trying to foal, and something must be wrong."

"Call Chandler," she said. "He's in the den."

"I've already tried. My phone is dead, and so is the landline."

"I don't have my phone with me. But I can run and get him," she offered as her gaze continued to dart frantically back and forth between him and the mare.

"No, there's no time for that!" He switched on the lantern and set it where it would be out of the way but still shed enough light for him to work by. "I want you to kneel down by her head and neck and gently stroke her. Speak to her softly, and try to reassure her while I see what I can do."

She did as he instructed, and Colt quickly examined the mare to assess the situation.

After a moment, Sophia asked, "Can you determine what's wrong?"

He let out a ragged breath. "Yes, the foal is positioned wrong. It can't come out. I'm going to have to get the mare up and walk her a bit. Then I might be able to turn the foal."

While he fastened a lead rope to Doll Brown's halter and urged the mare to stand, Sophia took his phone and attempted to call the house again.

"Still no signal," she said. "I can't believe this, Colt! It seems surreal that everyone is up there in the warm den, having a good time, and this emergency is going on here in the barn. And they don't even know it!"

"That's the way it is on a ranch sometimes, Sophia. Anything can happen at any given moment."

He led Doll Brown through several circles around the large stall, then made another search for the baby.

"Oh, thank God, I think I can turn it now." He darted a glance at Sophia, who was anxiously watching from a corner of the stall. "Send up a prayer, sweetheart, and hopefully you're about to see your first foal born."

"Don't worry," she told him, "I'll be praying the whole time."

He didn't have to urge Doll Brown to lie down; she seemed to know there wasn't any more time to dally around. Once she was on her side, Sophia attempted to soothe her, while Colt went to work repositioning the foal.

Although it was only a short minute or two before Colt finished the difficult task, to him it felt as if eons had passed before the baby finally slipped safely from the mare and onto the bed of clean straw.

"Oh, Colt, you've done it! There it is!" Sophia exclaimed. "Is it alive?"

"Yes, he's breathing. And so far Doll Brown isn't hemorrhaging." He gave the mare's hip a fond pat. "Good job, girl. You have a new Christmas baby."

He looked over to see Sophia was still stroking the mare's neck. At the same time, tears were streaming down her face, and the sight of them tore a hole right in his chest.

"Sophia?" He circled his arms around her, then slowly he rose and drew her to a standing position with him. He pressed her cheek to the middle of his chest and stroked his hand through her hair. "Don't cry. It's all over. Everything is going to be okay."

Her arms wrapped around his waist and clung tightly. "Oh, Colt, I've never seen anything so frightening or so very beautiful. Without your help, they would've died!"

He rubbed a hand against her back, while thinking he had his whole world right here in his arms, and he never intended to let her go.

"You're making me out to be a hero," he protested. "And all I did was what a thousand other ranchers would've done."

"I don't believe that. But you can believe this."

Tilting her head back, she gazed up at him through a wall of tears. "You are my hero, Colt. And I'm so sorry."

"You haven't done anything to be sorry for," he said gently.

"Yes, I have. That night in your house—after we made love I was…terrified. I kept thinking *I love this man—I love him—and he's going to break my heart!* All I wanted to do was run from you as fast as I could."

"And now? Looks like you've run right back to me," he said with a wry grin.

Her smile was wobbly. "Yes, right back to you. These past few days I came to realize a future without you would be meaningless. I love you, Colt."

"I love you, Sophia," he whispered. "And I'm sorry, too. Sorry that I didn't tell you that sooner. You talked about being afraid. Well, maybe I was a little scared, too. We hadn't known each other for very long, and suddenly I found myself falling in love. And I knew it had to be love because it was like nothing I'd ever felt before. I started imagining myself as your husband and the father of our children, and then I thought I was crazy for thinking a girl as pretty and sweet and smart as you would ever consider marrying a guy like me. You wouldn't, would you?"

A soft laugh rushed past her lips. "Is that a roundabout way of proposing? If it is, the answer is a definite yes."

Bending his head, he kissed her and all the while

he was trying to let his lips convey the enormity of his love, he felt that very same love from Sophia flowing right back at him.

When the kiss finally ended, Colt gazed solemnly into her eyes and gently stroked her cheek.

"I promise, sweetheart, that I will always be with you. And no matter how many babies you want to give me, whether that's two or ten, I'll be a happy man."

"You really want to be a father? You're not just saying that?"

He laughed with pure joy. "Are you kidding? Seems like all I do around here is deliver babies. It's about time I had some of my own."

Colt had barely gotten the words out when Doll Brown nickered softly, and they glanced over to see the foal had lifted its head and was enjoying a warm lick from his mother's tongue.

Tears welled in Sophia's eyes, but this time Colt understood they were born out of joy.

"Oh, my, they're quite a pair," she whispered.

"And so are we, darling. For now and always." He planted a kiss on her cheek. "Merry Christmas."

"Yes, and what a glorious Christmas it's going to be."

He wrapped his hand around hers. "I think it's safe for us to walk back to the house and let everyone know what's happened with us and the new foal. While we're gone, it will give Doll Brown and her baby a chance to bond. We'll come back in a few minutes and check on them."

She nodded. "Perhaps we should go. Someone might be missing us by now," she said. "And if your phone is dead, no one can call."

He pulled the phone from his pocket and promptly shook his head in amazement. "This makes no sense at all. The signal is as strong as ever now."

"Oh! Oh, Colt, look!" Sophia suddenly cried out.

Colt glanced around to see she was pointing up at the skylight situated high above the stall. A bright star was shining a brilliant light straight down to create a golden glow over the mare and baby.

Amazed by the sight, he whispered reverently, "Away in a manger."

"It's a miracle," she murmured, then turned and hugged herself tightly to him. "It's the Christmas Star shining down on them."

As Colt gathered her close in his arms, he said, "It's shining down on us, too, my love. Tonight, and all our nights to come."

Epilogue

Seven weeks later, on a mild February night, a fire was blazing in the firepit on the patio behind the ranch house. Strings of festive lights twinkled down from the roof, music played softly in the background, and Jazelle was busy handing out fluted glasses filled with expensive champagne.

On a low stone bench, not far from the crackling fire, Sophia sat close to Colt's side, but her gaze wasn't on him. Instead it was locked on the sparkling engagement ring on her finger.

A few days after he'd proposed to her on Christmas Eve, Colt had presented her with the beautiful engagement ring fashioned with a white, square cut diamond surrounded with smaller stones of the same color.

Now that Valentine's Day had arrived, the ring reminded her of how much her life had changed since she'd come to the ranch. Not only did she have her dream job with her grandmother, she was also going to marry the man she loved with all her heart. They were going to make a real home and a family together.

Drawing his face close to her ear, he murmured, "Are you happy with my Valentine's gift to you?"

Smiling, she reached up and touched one of the silver-and-turquoise earrings Colt had given her earlier today. "Oh yes! They're exactly what I wanted," she told him. "But at this very moment I just happened to be thinking about my engagement ring. It's beautiful. Especially because it symbolizes our love and commitment to each other."

A half grin lifted one corner of his lips. "It's beautiful because you're wearing it, sweetheart."

She pressed a kiss to his cheek. "Hmm. That's a very Valentine thing to say to me."

Lifting the hand wearing the engagement ring, he kissed the palm. "It might take a while, but you'll learn that us cowboys can be very romantic."

Lowering her lashes, she offered him a provocative little smile. "Is that right?"

"Very right," he said in a voice only she could

hear. "Once this party is over, I'll be happy to show you."

Sophia was about to whisper something naughty in his ear when Blake strolled up to them.

"Are you two enjoying the champagne? Mom doesn't usually break out the bubbly for Valentine's Day, but she wanted to honor your engagement."

Colt pointed to his and Sophia's emptied glasses. "We've already finished one glass. But I'm thinking it's about time for a second. Maureen must have dug out a good year. It's great."

"Well, you two have been engaged for a few weeks now," Blake said, "but I wanted to offer you both my congratulations again. And I have a question. Is this going to be a short or long engagement? Kat's been wondering whether to buy a new maternity dress for the wedding or a regular-sized one."

Since his wife, Katherine, had learned she was expecting twins in late summer, everyone had been teasing Blake about having double the trouble. But in truth, Sophia had never seen the man so happy.

"By the time I get the wedding plans made, Kat will be able to wear a svelte dress," Sophia answered before Colt had a chance.

"Sophia has it all wrong," Colt said, while giving his fiancée a calculating grin. "It's going to be a *very* short engagement. With only a small—well, kind of small—wedding."

"Yeah, kinda." Laughing, Blake jerked his thumb

toward the end of the patio where Maureen was wrapped snugly in the arm of her husband. "Good luck convincing Mom. You two know she'll insist on helping with the wedding plans. Before you know what's happened, she'll have at least three hundred people on the guest list and a whole roasted steer on the dinner menu."

Sophia and Colt exchanged uncertain glances, which only caused Blake to laugh again.

"Don't worry, she's already said she's footing the bill. You two should know she considers you family. We all do." He gave them a wink and then moved on across the patio to where his wife was reclining on a lounge chair.

Squeezing her hand, Colt said, "Sounds like we might as well get ready for a big blowout of a wedding."

"Does that idea bother you?" she asked.

"Not one bit. If you want a fancy, gigantic ceremony, then I want you to have it. And Maureen is like a mother to us. We don't want to disappoint her. Anyway, the important thing is you're going to be my wife, and that's all I care about."

She placed her hand alongside his face. "That's all I care about, too, Colt. You and me making a home together. I don't even care that my mother has already said she isn't coming to the wedding."

A rueful grimace turned down the corners of his mouth. "She probably considers a horseman as too low-life to be her daughter's husband. I don't care what she thinks of me. But are you sure her decision to stay away isn't hurting you?"

"Listen, Colt. Mom is staying away for many reasons. The major one being that, after the way she's disowned Reeva all these years, she's too ashamed to face her," Sophia said, then smiled to soften her words. "Gran loves you. That's more than enough blessing for me. And Dad has already promised to be here. I'm so looking forward to spending time with him. And to meeting your father."

"To be honest, Luke and I were both shocked that Dad has agreed to come out and spend a few days with us. It's the first we've ever known of him traveling for more than a day's drive, so the wedding is going to be a big deal for him."

"For all of us," she agreed.

He glanced thoughtfully around the patio where most of the family were milling about and enjoying the champagne. "The Hollisters have a way of bringing people together. Just look at us."

"I'm not sure if I've ever told you, but the night of the Christmas Eve party, Maureen literally grabbed my arm and hustled me out to the sleigh. She was determined to throw me at you." Sophia squeezed his hand. "I'm very grateful she refused to let me hide in the house. Otherwise, you might've given up on me and found yourself a new girlfriend."

"Ha! No chance. I was determined to put my

brand on you—no matter how long it took. I just
didn't know how I was going to convince you that I
seriously loved you. And then when I heard you calling to me in the barn, I knew everything was going
to be right with you and me."

"That was a night I'll never forget," she said, then
added with a tender smile, "It was magical. But, then,
every day with you is like a fairy tale come true."

He chuckled softly. "I wonder if you'll still call
it a fairy tale by the time we have our third child?"

"Only the third? I'll show you, cowboy. Even after
the sixth baby, I'll still be thinking of myself as the
real Cinderella."

The kiss she pressed to his cheek brought a smile
to his face. "A big family, huh? Sounds like we're
going to fit right in with the rest of the Hollisters."

Sophia glanced thoughtfully at Maureen and Gil.
"Speaking of big families, I heard some interesting
news today. As you might say, it came straight from
the horse's mouth."

His expression was dubious. "Whatever it is, it
couldn't be bigger news than our engagement."

She playfully pinched his arm. "I said *interesting*, not *bigger*."

"Okay. And what horse's mouth did you hear this
from?"

"Maureen herself. She ate lunch with me and
Gran. Seems she's decided that the Hollister fam-

ily has grown so large it's time for her to make a family tree."

"Wow! It's going to need some strong branches to hold up that many names," Colt said.

"It's possible there might be more names than we think," Sophia told him.

"What does that mean? Someone in the family besides Isabelle and Kat is pregnant?"

"Not that I know of. But Maureen has been digging into the genealogy of the family, and she says the name of Hadley Hollister keeps popping up."

Colt's brows arched with curiosity. "She doesn't know this person?"

"No. She has no idea if the man might be related. And frankly, she's torn over whether she should dig deeper into the matter or dismiss the whole idea that there might be more to this family of Hollisters than they know about."

"Hmm. Well, if there were more to the Crawford family out there, I'd probably want to know about them." He nuzzled his nose against the side of her hair. "But you know what? I'd much rather you and I just produce our own little Crawfords."

Unconcerned that anyone might be watching, Sophia turned his face toward hers and softly kissed his lips. "So would I, my darling."

* * * * *

And if you want more
Western-themed Christmas romances,
try these other great books:

Dreaming of a Christmas Cowboy
By Brenda Harlen

His Baby No Matter What
By Melissa Senate

The Cowboy's Christmas Retreat
By Catherine Mann

Available now wherever
Harlequin Special Edition books
and ebooks are sold!

WE HOPE YOU ENJOYED
THIS BOOK FROM

HARLEQUIN
SPECIAL
EDITION

Believe in love. Overcome obstacles. Find happiness.

Relate to finding comfort and strength in the
support of loved ones and enjoy the journey
no matter what life throws your way.

6 NEW BOOKS AVAILABLE EVERY MONTH!

#2881 THEIR NEW YEAR'S BEGINNING
The Fortunes of Texas: The Wedding Gift • by Michelle Major

Brian Fortune doesn't think he will ever find the woman he kissed at his brother's New Year's wedding. So when the search for the provenance of a mysterious gift leads him into a local antique store a few days later, he's stunned to find Emmaline Lewis, proprietor—and mystery kisser! Brian has never been the type to commit, but suddenly he knows he'd do anything to stay at Emmaline's side—for good.

#2882 HER HOMETOWN MAN
Sutton's Place • by Shannon Stacey

Summoned home by her mother and sisters, novelist Gwen Sutton has made it clear—she's not staying. She's returning to her quiet life as soon as the family brewery is up and running. But when Case Danforth offers his help, it's clear there's more than just beer brewing! Time is short for Case to convince Gwen that a home with him is where her heart is.

#2883 THE RANCHER'S BABY SURPRISE
Texas Cowboys & K-9s • by Sasha Summers

Former soldier John Mitchell has come home after being discharged and asks to stay with his best friend, Natalie. They're both in for a shock when a precious baby girl is left on Natalie's doorstep—and John is the father! Now John needs Natalie's help more than ever. But Natalie has been in love with John forever. How can she help him find his way to being a family man if she's not part of that family?

#2884 THE CHARMING CHECKLIST
Charming, Texas • by Heatherly Bell

Max Del Toro persuaded his friend Ava Long to play matchmaker in exchange for posing as her boyfriend for one night. He even gave her a list of must-haves for his future wife. Except now he can't stop thinking about Ava—who doesn't check a single item on his list!

#2885 HIS LOST AND FOUND FAMILY
Sierra's Web • by Tara Taylor Quinn

Learning he's guardian to his orphaned niece sends architect Michael O'Connell's life into a tailspin. He's floored by the responsibility, so when Mariah Anderson agrees to pitch in at home, Michael thinks she's heaven-sent. He's shocked at the depth of his own connection to Mariah and opens his heart to her in ways he never imagined. But can an instant family turn into a forever one?

#2886 A CHEF'S KISS
Small Town Secrets • by Nina Crespo

Small-town chef Philippa Gayle's onetime rival-turned-lover Dominic Crawford upended her life. But when she's forced together with the celebrity cook on a project that could change her life, there's no denying that the flames that were lit years ago were only banked, not extinguished. Can Philippa trust Dominic enough to let him in...or are they just cooking up another heartbreak?

SPECIAL EXCERPT FROM

HARLEQUIN
SPECIAL EDITION

*Brian Fortune doesn't think he will ever find the
woman he kissed at his brother's New Year's wedding.
So when the search for the provenance of a mysterious
gift leads him into a local antique store a few days
later, he's stunned to find Emmaline Lewis, proprietor—
and mystery kisser! Brian has never been the type to
commit—but suddenly he knows he'll do anything to
stay at Emmaline's side—for good...*

*Read on for a sneak peek of the first book in the
The Fortunes of Texas: The Wedding Gift continuity,
Their New Year's Beginning,
by USA TODAY bestselling author Michelle Major!*

"I'd like to take you out on a proper date then."

"Okay." Color bloomed in her cheeks. "That would be
nice." He leaned in, but she held up a finger. "You should
know that since Kirby and the gang outed my pregnancy
at the coffee shop, I'm not going to hide it anymore." She
pressed a hand to her belly. "I'm wearing a baggy shirt
tonight because it seemed easier than fielding questions
from the boys, but if we go out, there will be questions.
And comments."

"I don't care about what anyone else thinks," he
assured her and then kissed her gently. "This is about you
and me."

Get 4 FREE REWARDS!

We'll send you 2 FREE Books <u>plus</u> 2 FREE Mystery Gifts.

Harlequin Special Edition books relate to finding comfort and strength in the support of loved ones and enjoying the journey no matter what life throws your way.

FREE Value Over **$20**

Those must have been the right words, because Emmaline wound her arms around his neck and drew closer. "I'm glad," she said, but before he could kiss her again, she yawned once more.

"I'll walk you to your car."

She mock pouted but didn't argue. "I'm definitely not as fun as I used to be," she told him as he picked up the bags with the leftover supplies to carry for her. "Actually I'm not sure I was ever that fun."

"As far as I'm concerned, you're the best."

After another lingering kiss, Emmaline climbed into her car and drove away. Brian watched her taillights until they disappeared around a bend. The night sky overhead was once again filled with stars, and he breathed in the fresh Texas air. He needed to stay in the moment and remember his reason for being in town and how long he planned to stay. He knew better than to examine the feeling of contentment coursing through him.

One thing he knew for certain was that it couldn't last.

Don't miss
Their New Year's Beginning *by Michelle Major,*
available January 2022 wherever
Harlequin Special Edition books and ebooks are sold.

Harlequin.com

He felt rather than witnessed her shrug. The same with the small kiss she pressed to the middle of his shoulder blades. He locked his muscles, forcing his head not to fall back. Ordering his throat to imprison the moan scrabbling up from his chest. Commanding his dick to stand down.

"Because you needed me," she said.

So simple. So goddamn true.

He did need her. Her friendship. Her body.

Her heart.

But since he could only have one of those, he'd take it. With a woman like her—generous, sweet, beautiful of body and spirit—even part of her was preferable to none of her. And if he dared to profess his true feelings, that was exactly what he would be left with. None of her. Their friendship would be ruined, and she was too important to him to risk losing her.

Carefully, he turned and wrapped her in his embrace, shielding her from the night air. Convincing himself if this was all he could have of her—even if it meant Gavin would have all of her—then he would be okay, he murmured, "You're really going to have to remove 'rescue best friend' off your résumé. For one, it's beginning to get too time-consuming. And two, the cape clashes with your gown."

She chuckled against his chest, tipping her head back to smile up at him. He curled his fingers against her spine, but that didn't prevent the ache to trace that sensual bottom curve.

"Where would be the fun in that? You're stuck with me, Kenan. And I'm stuck with you. Friends forever."

Friends.

The sweet sting of that knife buried between his ribs.

"Always, sweetheart."

Don't miss what happens next in
The Perfect Fake Date *by Naima Simone,*
the next book in the Billionaires of Boston series!

Available January 2022 wherever
Harlequin Desire books and ebooks are sold.

Harlequin.com

SPECIAL EXCERPT FROM

⊕ HARLEQUIN

DESIRE

Learning he's the secret heir to a business mogul,
Kenan Rhodes has a lot to prove. His best friend,
lingerie designer Eve Burke, agrees to work with him...
if he'll help her sharpen her dating skills.
Soon, fake dates lead to sexy nights...

Read on for a sneak peek of
The Perfect Fake Date,
by USA TODAY *bestselling author Naima Simone.*

The corridor ended, and he stood in front of another set of towering doors. Kenan briefly hesitated, then grasped the handle, opened the doors and slipped through to the balcony beyond. The cool April night air washed over him. The calendar proclaimed spring had arrived, but winter hadn't yet released its grasp over Boston, especially at night. But he welcomed the chilled breeze over his face, let it seep beneath the confines of his tuxedo to the hot skin below. Hoped it could cool the embers of his temper...the still-burning coals of his hurt.

"For someone who is known as the playboy of Boston society, you sure will ditch a party in a hot second." Slim arms slid around him, and he closed his eyes in pain and pleasure as the petite, softly curved body pressed to his back. "All I had to do was follow the trail of longing glances from the women in the hall to figure out where you'd gone."

He snorted. "Do you lie to your mama with that mouth? There was hardly anyone out there."

"Fine," Eve huffed. "So I didn't go with the others and watched all of that go down with your parents and brother. I waited until you left the ballroom and went after you."

"Why?" he rasped.